SPECIAL MESSAGE TO READERS

THE ULVERSCROFT FOUNDATION
(registered UK charity number 264873)
was established in 1972 to provide funds for research, diagnosis and treatment of eye diseases.
Examples of major projects funded by the Ulverscroft Foundation are:-

- The Children's Eye Unit at Moorfields Eye Hospital, London
- The Ulverscroft Children's Eye Unit at Great Ormond Street Hospital for Sick Children
- Funding research into eye diseases and treatment at the Department of Ophthalmology, University of Leicester
- The Ulverscroft Vision Research Group, Institute of Child Health
- Twin operating theatres at the Western Ophthalmic Hospital, London
- The Chair of Ophthalmology at the Royal Australian College of Ophthalmologists

You can help further the work of the Foundation by making a donation or leaving a legacy. Every contribution is gratefully received. If you would like to help support the Foundation or require further information, please contact:

THE ULVERSCROFT FOUNDATION
The Green, Bradgate Road, Anstey
Leicester LE7 7FU, England
Tel: (0116) 236 4325

website: www.foundation.ulverscroft.com

RAYMOND HAIGH

SISTER SLAUGHTER

Complete and Unabridged

ULVERSCROFT
Leicester

First published in Great Britain in 2013 by
Robert Hale Limited
London

First Large Print Edition
published 2015
by arrangement with
Robert Hale Limited
London

*A catalogue record for this book is available
from the British Library.*

ISBN 978–1–4448–2469–8

Published by
F. A. Thorpe (Publishing)
Anstey, Leicestershire

Set by Words & Graphics Ltd.
Anstey, Leicestershire
Printed and bound in Great Britain by
T. J. International Ltd., Padstow, Cornwall

This book is printed on acid-free paper

1

The man was here again today, hiding amongst the trees, staring intently at the house. Yesterday he'd arrived in the evening, not the morning, and he'd stood further around the edge of the wood so he could look at the wing with the bricked-up windows.

Zarina settled her slender hips more comfortably between the roots of the massive tree and studied him. Oily black hair and a swarthy complexion, somewhat darker than hers; a drab green bomber jacket and brown trousers that made him almost invisible amongst the leaves and branches — perhaps he'd chosen his clothing with that in mind.

She watched him tug down a zip and slide something from his jacket. A sudden breeze made leaves tremble; sunbeams flickered, and the light shimmered on whatever it was he was holding. She narrowed her eyes. It was a camera, black and complicated-looking. He lifted it to his face and peered into the view-finder while he fiddled with the lens.

The murmur of an engine grew louder; tyres drummed over uneven paving. Zarina turned and glanced towards the house. The nurse's little yellow car was rolling to a stop beside the front steps. It was the dark-haired nurse this morning, smart in her crisp blue and white uniform, her little white hat pinned to her hair. She looked a bit like one of the nurses in those funny *Carry On* films her mother didn't like her to watch. Zarina felt a pang of envy. The nurse was grown up. She'd got her life sorted. She was important and independent, not lonely and abandoned and frightened. She heard the camera shutter going click, click, click as the nurse took her bag and a brown paper parcel from the back of the car, climbed the steps and disappeared through the big entrance door.

The man was concealing the camera inside his jacket now. When he tugged up the zip, he glanced towards her. Her body tensed. For a moment she thought he'd seen her, but he just turned and set off through the trees, heading in the direction of the mausoleum.

Zarina didn't think he had anything to do with the men who watched the gates and walked around the grounds. They wore baggy dark-blue uniforms with heavy sleeveless jackets and close-fitting caps, like baseball caps, with the shades pulled down to hide their eyes. Their boots were big, with thick rubber soles, and a lot of small pouches were clipped to their belts. Sometimes they carried guns. When they came close she could hear the hiss and crackle of their two-way radios; their muttered conversations.

Her world, her safe secure little world, had ended the day those people came and took her mother and brother and sister away. Before Alexander, before little Amir and Maria, when she'd lived in Egypt, her mother had said to her, 'Run away and hide if the police come. Whatever happens to me or your grandmother or your Uncle Asheya, don't let them catch you or they'll take you away and do bad things to you.'

When she'd asked her mother what the bad things were, she'd said, 'They'll take off your clothes and bind your hands and feet to a pole — they call it the chicken — then they'll do things to you that you are too young to understand.' She'd asked why they would do these things and her mother had said, 'Because you are a girl, who will soon begin to look like a woman, and you are a Christian and the police hate Christians.'

What her mother had told her had scared her. It had given her bad dreams. So, when they came that day and the two women had carried Amir and Maria over to their car and her mother had begun to shout and scream, she'd run into the trees and watched. Her mother had fought the women. She'd punched and kicked and bitten and scratched and torn out handfuls of hair, and the big policeman had grabbed her mother, pulled her arms behind her back and held them while the policewoman fastened her wrists. Then they'd dragged her, kicking and screaming, to a white car with a blue and yellow stripe and pushed her inside. The white car had led the way when they left, its siren howling, its blue light flashing. That was the last she'd seen of her mother and her little brother and sister.

After they'd gone, she'd plunged into the wood, wading through bracken until she was hidden amongst the bushes and undergrowth behind the mausoleum. She'd waited there for ages before heading back. A blue van marked *Beckminster Borough Council Social Services Department* had been parked by the steps. She'd crept around the side of the house, keeping her head down and her body close to the wall so they wouldn't see her if they were looking out of the windows. A quick dash across the deserted rear yard, past the old stable block and down the gloomy scullery passage, got her into the kitchen. Pans were boiling over on the battered old Aga cooker, and there were potato peelings in a bowl on the table.

She'd tiptoed down the kitchen corridor;

emerged in the hall. Women's voices were echoing down the stairs. Alexander's bedroom door was open. He was moaning and crying, and there were terrible sounds of someone coughing and being sick. Then the door had opened wider and a dark-suited, bald-headed man had stepped out. One of those doctors' things — pink rubber and silvery tubes — was clipped around his neck, and he was carrying a black bag. He'd talked into a mobile phone while he thudded down the stairs.

She'd darted behind one of the big marble columns, edged around it, keeping herself hidden while he'd crossed the hall. 'He's very ill,' she'd heard him saying. 'He's alone in the house and there's only a half-witted gardener-cum-handyman in the grounds. You've taken his wife away, so you'll have to send care workers in.' Then he'd listened for a moment before snapping angrily, 'No I can't get him a bed in Beckminster General. Anyway, he'd probably refuse to go. It's terminal. It would only be for a week — ten days at the most. There's a couple of carers with him now, but he needs night and day cover.' He paused to listen, then, more angrily, 'Don't talk to me about spending cuts. You've taken his wife and kids away. You've caused the problem. Put someone in.'

From behind the column, she'd watched him pocket his phone, tug the tube thing from around his neck and toss it into his bag before crashing out through the front door. After he'd gone, she'd crept up the stairs and peered into Alexander's room. She wished she hadn't. It had reeked of sick and poo and Alexander was moaning and crying out with pain. Two elderly women dressed in green overalls, one on either side of the bed, were trying to roll him onto a blue plastic sheet. Soiled bed-clothes were strewn all over the floor. 'Sorry, love, I'm sorry, love,' they kept saying, 'but we've got to move you. We've got to get you cleaned up. We can't leave you like this.'

She'd run back down the stairs, through the deserted kitchen and out into the sunlight and the clean-smelling summer air. Afraid she might be taken away too, she'd not dared to go into the house again. She'd slept in the tiny slopey-ceilinged attic above Nathan's bothy in the rear yard. He'd shared his meals with her, and she'd spent the days roaming the grounds and the disused quarry, always on the lookout for the men in baggy blue uniforms. Much of the time she'd sat quietly between the roots of the old tree, watching rabbits feed on the greenery in a clearing; watching all the comings and goings to and from the house.

They didn't bring her mother back, or her brother, or her sister. She'd tried to keep count of the days since they'd been taken away, but she'd got in a muddle. On the second day, a man had called. Big and tall, a bit red-faced, dressed in a dark suit with a red and blue striped tie. He'd looked very smart — like Alexander when he walked out with her mother — and he'd worn a hat. A fedora? Mmm . . . no, not one of those small American things. This had a wider brim — not a homburg — a trilby. That was it, a trilby: pale grey with a broad black band. And he'd worn grey leather driving gloves and carried an old briefcase. He'd climbed the steps and tugged at the bell pull, then waited a long time because the bell hadn't worked for ages. Eventually he'd banged on the door and one of the women in green overalls had opened it. It was quiet here, and from across the forecourt she could hear his deep and very refined voice saying, 'Soames: Major Marcus Soames. Professor Meyer is expecting me.' Then he'd taken off his hat and stepped inside.

The women in green overalls didn't come the next day, or the days after that. Instead, three nurses came: one blonde, one with red hair, the other with brown. All very pretty, all wearing those blue and white uniforms and tiny white hats. As one left another one arrived: very early in the morning, at lunch time and in the evening, usually before she went over to Nathan's bothy and climbed the ladder to her bed in the attic.

On the fourth or fifth day, two women and the police had come back to the house. The one who'd fought with her mother, the one who'd lost a lot of hair, wasn't with them; another woman, dark-haired and smartly dressed, had come in her place. They spent a long time inside, then the police brought Nathan round to the front and the women came out and tried to question him about a missing child, a child called Zarina. They'd been searching for *her*.

Nathan had just snuffled and grunted and grinned, the way he did when someone embarrassed or upset him. His ears couldn't hear sounds, and his mouth couldn't make words, but he'd have known from their lips what they were saying.

In the end, the policeman and policewoman had started to smile and the two other women had become angry. They just gave up, climbed back in their cars and drove away.

Zarina sighed. She missed Alexander. She wanted him almost as badly as she wanted her mother. He was patient and gentle with her, made her feel grown up, allowed her to see and touch the fascinating things in the big air-conditioned storeroom with the bricked-up windows, let her read the books in his library — sometimes she'd curl up with a book on the big leather sofa while he worked at his desk. And he'd made her mother so happy, brought them to his house in England where he said they'd all be safe; somehow he knew that the revolution was coming, that it would make Egypt a dangerous place for them. He couldn't have known that England would become a dangerous place for them, too.

She still missed the heat, the brightness of the light, the vivid colours, the little school where she was taught by nuns and boys weren't allowed to be cruel and rude. She missed the bustle of the bazaars, the cries of the muezzin from the minarets, the sounds and smells of Cairo. But she'd been happy in this green and quiet place, and she'd been glad to put a big distance between herself and her Uncle Asheya.

Zarina held up dirt-ingrained fingers and began to count. Eight, nine — it had been more than ten days since her mother and little brother and sister had been taken away. Tears began to prickle behind her eyes. She mustn't cry. Crying was a waste of time when there was no one to hear, but she wanted her old life back so desperately.

Her bottom was cold. She could feel the dampness of the earth through the seat of her jeans. Nathan would be up and about now, washing himself at the pump in the stable yard. She wiped her eyes and rose to her feet. She'd go and ask him to fry bacon for sandwiches while she sliced bread and made them mugs of tea.

Suddenly remembering, she patted the pocket of her shirt. It was still there: the hank of hair attached to a patch of bloody skin. If she could pluck up the courage to creep into Alexander's library, carry the ladder over to the shelves near the door and climb up to the top, she could take down one of the books that would tell her how to use it.

2

A sudden breeze, warm on her bare arms and shoulders, rippled the tassels on the awnings above the tables and brought with it a fragrance of roses from the surrounding gardens. Samantha breathed in the cloyingly sweet scent. Oblivious to her companion, she was leafing through the contents of a dark-green folder, skim-reading pages of double-spaced type, working her way towards photographs in a pocket at the back.

Marcus Soames drew gently on the remains of his cigar, slowly exhaled, then studied her through the haze of smoke. Her usually creamy-white skin was evenly tanned. Her gleaming black hair — abundant, straight, not quite shoulder-length — fell across her brow in a deep fringe. Even he could tell it had been expertly cut and styled. He puffed on his cigar. 'Take your valet, your hairdresser, with you to Italy, Sam?'

'Crispin isn't my valet, Marcus. Only men have valets. But he does wash and cut my hair, and we did go on holiday together.' She didn't bother to look up from the typewritten sheets.

'Your manservant, then,' Marcus conceded. 'Must say, he's looking after you extremely well.'

'He's not my manservant, Marcus, he's my dearest friend. We've had this conversation before, and you should know by now that I resent you mocking him.'

Marcus chuckled. 'Not mocking the man. Wouldn't dream of it. I'm only saying he's doing a wonderful job. Did he choose the dress?'

Samantha turned a page. 'He did, Marcus. He discovered it in a little boutique in Rome: Bottega Veneta's spring collection, if you're interested. He's got an eye for colour.'

'Who's got an eye, Crispin or Bottega?'

'Crispin. He was very taken by the way the blue deepens from azure on the bodice to ultramarine around the hem.'

Marcus exhaled; another puff of smoke. 'Man's a godsend. Don't know what you'd do without him.' He chuckled throatily.

'You really are annoying me now, Marcus. I don't like the way you demean Crispin. He's a kind and gentle friend who's very sweet to me. I love him dearly.'

Marcus, suitably chastened, relaxed back in his chair and studied what there was of the blue dress that had delighted Crispin. Silk, he decided, that would explain why it was so clingy. And, even to his uneducated eye, it was beautifully made and strikingly elegant. He went on puffing his cigar while his wickedly blue eyes, narrowing in the smoke, continued to study the woman who was engrossed in the documents he'd brought her. Her breasts were high and taut and full; but not, he reflected, excessively full. A blue bootlace strap was about to slide over her shoulder. There were no other straps, no signs of any underwear. Could she be wearing one of those things his wife wore with her off-the-shoulder evening gown: a sort of corset that fastened around the back? He remembered following Samantha to their table. The back of the dress had plunged to the waist and the expanse of tanned skin hadn't been traversed by any straps. Perhaps her breasts were simply nestling there, unsupported, free and unrestrained beneath the silk. He sighed. What a sublime thought.

Samantha glanced up. Marcus flinched. Those eyes: so huge, so green, so chillingly remote. It was like having an ice pick rammed into one's brain. He watched crimson lips part in a smile: she hadn't been offended by him staring at her like that; she wasn't prudish.

Returning her smile, he asked softly, 'Why, Sam?'

'Why what?'

'Why a man like Crispin?'

'I thought I'd explained. He's gentle and kind, sensitive to my moods, and — '

'I understand all that.'

'What, then?' She didn't keep the irritation from her voice.

'There's no future in it, Sam.'

'Does there have to be? And the way I live, I may not have a future. I love him, Marcus. He's just so pleasant and relaxing to be with. When we're on holiday he keeps lecherous men at bay, and he's so outrageously handsome all the women are jealous.'

'I'd have thought he'd have been something of a man-magnet,' Marcus muttered.

'I don't have any problems with the kind of men he attracts.'

He ground the stub of his cigar in an ashtray, exhaled smoke, then said gently, 'It's been eight years, Sam.'

'Nine, Marcus.'

'Eight, nine; it's a long time to be — '

'I can't help the way I feel. And there's Agape as well as Eros. Love isn't just about sex.'

'And is Crispin still convinced you're an expensive call girl?'

'I *am* an expensive call girl,' she snapped back. 'You pay me well and I'm always at your beck and call.'

'I mean, does he still think men pay you for sex?'

'Of course. It's a conclusion he reached soon after we met: the days spent away from home, the clothes, the car, the holidays. And I lie to him, tell him how tiresome the clients have been, maintain the deception, avoid the awful reality.' Suddenly she understood. This wasn't idle, prurient curiosity; he was concerned about security. She gave him a reassuring smile. 'Don't worry, Marcus. Crispin poses no threat. I'd have much more to lose than you if anyone discovered my secrets. And he's no hang-ups about a woman selling her body for sex — he's broken too many taboos himself — but he'd run a mile if he knew I dealt in death.'

Reassured, Marcus let it go. There were no problems — not for him, anyway. Her relationship with Crispin might be strange, but her cold and enduring anger had made her ruthless and deadly. Like old Alexander, she'd been very useful to him. More than useful; indispensable. He allowed his gaze to wander over smooth tanned shoulders and slender arms, the delicate hands with nails painted the same vivid red as her lips. How on earth did she hold that huge automatic pistol? She must have had the grip modified, but the sheer weight of it . . .

He suddenly thought of his wife, Charlotte. Plump arms, pink cheeks, heavy thighs, small pudding-bowl breasts: rather like those Picasso nudes in that gallery in Paris. There was nothing exotic about Charlotte. She was a very down to earth girl, a bishop's daughter, the mother of his two daughters, a woman who reared rare breeds of sheep. He neglected her dreadfully. He really must try to get home to the farm more often.

Returning his attention to the shapes beneath Samantha's dress, he suddenly thought: *What an unspeakable waste!* And the gleaming hair, the perfect face with its succulent mouth, the soft husky voice: they were utterly beguiling, too. But not her eyes. He wouldn't care to wake up with those strange, almost animal eyes gazing into his. And the horrendous things she'd done to men; the unimaginable pain she'd inflicted. He shuddered inwardly. How much vengeance did she want?

Samantha read through the last of the typewritten sheets, then turned to the glossy black and white photographs. She held one up. 'I take it this is Alexander Meyer?'

Marcus nodded.

'And he's . . . ' she glanced down at the notes, ' . . . professor of Ancient Egyptian studies at Cairo University?'

'Was. He resigned the post when he came back to England.'

'He looks very distinguished in that intellectual kind of way, and he's almost as handsome as you, Marcus. Is he very well known?'

'Well known and highly regarded. Visiting professor at Yale, lectured at the Sorbonne and Cambridge, used to be principal adviser to the Egyptian Ministry of Antiquities. Done the definitive translations of a lot of scrolls and inscriptions. Returned to England with his wife and children about three years ago. He knew the revolution was coming and he decided to get out. Came back to the family home: Sourbeck Hall. It's in Shropshire.'

Samantha picked out a photograph of a dark-skinned, dark-eyed woman with long dark hair that was tightly curled. She held it up.

Marcus drained his brandy glass. 'His wife, Rasha.'

'She's very beautiful.'

'Photograph hardly does her justice. She's a good deal younger than Alexander. She was a dancer — toast of Cairo.'

'What kind of dancer?'

'Classical. I think the Egyptians call it *raks sharki*.'

'She was a belly-dancer?'

Marcus's blue eyes twinkled. 'Important part of their artistic tradition; high-culture, completely respectable.'

'It's belly-dancing, Marcus. You say she was the toast of Cairo?'

'And Alexandria. Kimberley at the Foreign Office used to go and watch her dance when he was stationed at the embassy. He said it was utterly mesmerizing; sex set to music.' Marcus nodded towards the folder on Samantha's lap. 'There's a swatch of photographs of her in there somewhere.'

Samantha fished in the pocket at the back of the file and took out a bundle of what looked like postcards. She unfastened a tape and unfolded a ribbon of images.

'Mementos for the audience,' Marcus said, 'sold in the foyers of nightclubs and theatres where she performed. Kimberley let us have those for the file.'

Samantha studied the photographs. The professor's wife had generous breasts, a narrow waist and broad hips. Her dancer's legs were long and shapely. 'Voluptuous,' Samantha murmured. 'Very alluring in her harem pants and bangles. And her Wings-of-Isis outfit is absolutely stunning.' She refolded the images and slid them back into the file. 'What is it that you want me to do?'

'Go to Sourbeck Hall, stay with Alexander. Watch him, talk to him and note what he says until he dies. He's terminally ill: cancer. They think it might have started to spread.'

'It's not really my thing, Marcus, caring for the terminally ill.'

'I've arranged for nurses to go in, round-the-clock cover in three shifts.' He gestured towards the folder. Samantha passed it over the table. He took some seven-by-four colour photographs from an envelope and slid them across to her.

Samantha spread them out on the cloth. 'Very smart uniforms, Marcus. You don't see nurses looking like that any more. And all so attractive. Where did you find them?'

'The girls or the uniforms?'

'Both.'

'The girls are ours, on the payroll, full security clearance. The uniforms came from a medical clothing supplier along the Hammersmith Road. Seems they still wear things like that in some private hospitals and nursing homes. I suppose I was doing my best for old Alexander — giving him the pleasure of being cared for by pretty girls while he's still able to appreciate it. The nurses are staying in what was an officer's house on an airbase about seven miles from the Hall.'

'And how does Mrs Meyer feel about her

husband being cared for by all these pretty girls?'

'She's gone; taken the children with her. Alexander wasn't all that coherent when I visited, but I gather she left without warning. Probably couldn't cope with his illness. He's devastated; absolutely no idea where she is. He's afraid she might have gone back to Egypt and he doesn't much like the thought of that.'

'The girls: I take it they really are nurses?'

'State registered. One's a bit rusty, but the others support her. And the care's being supervised by the medical officer on the base — he's a doctor, of course. I suppose he'll become more involved as the illness progresses. And I've arranged for a woman from the village to go in and cook meals and manage the house; she's there from about seven 'til seven. Rasha used to do all the cooking, Egyptian style. When she left, the council sent in care workers twice a day. They stopped coming when the nurses came on the scene. The cook persuaded another woman from the village to go in most mornings and do some cleaning; it's a large old house that's a bit run down, so she can't do much, but she keeps the bathrooms and kitchen clean, tidies Alexander's bedroom, that sort of thing.'

Samantha shuffled the photographs together

and slid them over the table. 'You've gone to a great deal of trouble and expense, Marcus.'

'We owe it to the man. He's been invaluable to us over the years. Egypt's a gateway between Africa and Europe, a country where Alexander mingled with the great and the corrupt. He heard things, fed us information, all of it reliable. And he was particularly close to officials in the Ministry for Antiquities. He put money-making opportunities their way, and they made sure he got export licences. He's built up quite a collection over the years, all of it legitimately acquired, all of it with provenance. It's stored in a big air-conditioned annexe at the back of the Hall. Worth a fortune.' Marcus slid the file back across the table.

Samantha didn't bother to retrieve it. Instead, she picked up her cup and gazed at Marcus over the rim while she sipped at the now tepid coffee. His dark-blue pinstripe suit had been pressed, his shirt and pocket handkerchief freshly laundered, his Guards officer's tie was new-looking. She noticed more grey in his dark hair, his face seemed more florid and there were some broken veins on the bridge of his nose. Too many lavish expense-account lunches, like the one they'd just enjoyed, and too many brandies and cigars were helping his body to thicken into middle age; but his height, his broad shoulders, his military bearing, gave him great presence.

'I still don't understand why you want to involve me, Marcus.'

'When Alexander came back to England he promised me a detailed report on the contacts he'd had and the things he knew that had given him leverage. That's not quite so vital now, but some of the old faces are creeping back into power, so it could still be useful. The important thing is, he was going to set down the names, routes and places involved in the movement of South American drugs across Africa and into Europe. Al-Qaeda's getting a tighter hold on things since the Arab Spring, and that's worrying. We need the information.'

'You've already put nurses in there, Marcus; your people, people who'll be with him round the clock. Why do you need me?'

'Information gathering's not their game, Sam. And they don't speak Arabic. He rambles on in Arabic for much of the time. And you have a good knowledge of many things. You could talk to him about more than the weather and his state of health. You could persuade him to tell us what he knows; make notes, report back. We'd study what you were sending and feed you questions.'

Samantha gave him a dubious look.

He responded with a coaxing smile, then pushed the file a little further towards her. 'Just a couple of weeks, Sam. He can't live much longer than that. And he's quite charming; absolutely fascinating to talk to.' Wickedly blue eyes were smiling across at her.

'He's not the only one who's charming, Marcus, but my contract ends at midnight on Friday.'

'We'd renew.'

'Has Fallon sanctioned all this? I'm talking about the cost: three nurses, a cook, a cleaner, me.'

'Cost's always a problem, but the information he has is absolutely vital to us, and he has to be cared for and kept alive long enough for us to find out what he knows.'

'Left it a bit late, haven't you? From what you say, there could be very little time.'

'We've got to try. Loretta's peeved because we didn't get the information out of him months ago. Problem was, we'd no idea he was ill. I did my best to set something up, went to see him a number of times, but he kept putting me off. Looking back, I think he suspected that when he'd told us what he knew, I'd abandon him.'

'And would you have?'

'Absolutely not.' Marcus was indignant. 'He's served us well over the years. Must say, though, I'm disappointed he didn't trust me. I suppose it was fear. He'd have realized that changes after the revolution might leave him in need of protection. He was probably retaining the information as a bargaining counter.'

'Protection?'

'I've sent men in to guard the house and patrol the grounds; three Specials.'

The blue bootlace strap finally slid down Samantha's arm. She eased it back over her shoulder. 'You're not telling me everything, Marcus. Why does he need protection?'

'Many of the people he dealt with and socialized with, people who gossiped and were indiscreet, will have been rounded up and questioned, possibly tortured, by the new regime. Powerful men will have been made aware that his knowledge represents a personal threat to them and a threat to the trade that makes them rich. And the traffickers, the men who run the drug cartels, must be worried. They'll be hurt badly if we disturb the supply routes through Africa. He made no secret of where he was going when he left Egypt. They're not likely to know he's close to death, but they'll have no difficulty finding him. They might try to silence him.'

Samantha toyed with her coffee spoon. As usual, there was more to this than Marcus had cared to reveal, but she'd spent a fortune on clothes and holidaying with Crispin. Another contract was very tempting. 'You'd extend on the same terms, for six months?'

Marcus nodded. 'A year if you'd prefer.'

She picked up the file. 'Let's make it six months. When do you want me to go?'

'Today. I can phone the housekeeper, ask her to lay another place for dinner, get you a room ready. A nurse called Josie Stockwell is doing the afternoon shift this week. You'd be dining with her; she'd appreciate the company.'

'And what am I called?'

'Better use the name on your ID documents: Georgina Grey. Alexander's expecting someone by that name.'

Samantha couldn't help smiling. 'You were pretty sure I'd say yes.'

'It's a generous contract, Sam, and you've never let me down before.'

* * *

Zarina clambered up to the floor of the old saw house, leaned back against the remains of the steam engine that once powered the huge stone cutters and gazed down at her handiwork. It was better now, much better. This time, the circle she'd drawn on the flat shelf of rock was quite perfect. Trapping one end of her skipping rope beneath a heavy stone and holding the chalk against the other end while she swung it round had done the trick. If she'd thought of that a week ago, the magic would have been working by now. Or it would have if she'd had one of the old leather-bound books from the top shelf of Alexander's library.

About a year ago, before Alexander had become really ill, she'd climbed up the mahogany and brass ladder and carried one down: *The Key of Solomon.* She'd spent more than an hour utterly absorbed in it, then Alexander had come in and taken it from her. He'd told her it dealt with occult and mysterious things that young ladies shouldn't even know about, let alone concern themselves with. It was the first time he'd ever taken a book from her, and most of his books were about very grown-up things.

She remembered the bits about circles and pentagrams, remembered that they should be marked out with newly milled flour, but she couldn't remember any of the spells and invocations, and she didn't have any flour. And anyway, she wouldn't care to go to all this trouble, marking out a circle, only to have it washed away by the rain. So she'd taken a half-empty tin of bright-red paint from Nathan's workshop in the old stables and used a twig to dab and smear it along the chalk line. Perhaps white paint would have looked more like flour, but there wasn't any, and anyway, red represented Mars and she knew from one of Alexander's books that Mars was the ruler of Aries and Aries was her mother's birth sign.

Zarina felt her bottom lip trembling, felt that awful weepy sadness settling over her. It always did whenever she thought about her mother. She was beginning to lose hope now, beginning to fear that her mother and her brother and sister might never come back. What would she do then? Nathan had been kind to her, fed her, allowed her to sleep in the tiny attic room above his bothy, but she needed someone she could talk to, someone who could buy her new clothes, or at least sort out some clean ones. Nathan didn't understand things like that. Even if she plucked up the courage to creep into the house, she wouldn't dare go to her room and look for clothes. The nurses would be up there, caring for Alexander. They'd catch her and call the police, and the women would come and take her away.

But she had to go in and get one of those

books. It would be good to take them all, but they were so big and heavy she couldn't carry them. There were three, all leather bound, two of them with metal fastenings, and the one called *Grimorium Verum* had had its clasps fastened and locked. She'd hoped to creep into the house today, in the drowsy heat of the early afternoon, just after the nurses had changed over, but there'd been so many comings and goings she'd been too afraid to try.

The man with the camera had been again. She'd been sitting quietly, watching the rabbits, when he'd appeared through the trees. He'd crouched down in the bracken beyond the clearing. Secure in her hiding place, she'd watched him for a while, then she'd become drowsy. The faint click, click, click, of his camera had roused her and sent the rabbits scampering for their burrows. She'd followed his gaze towards the house and watched a black-haired woman swing her legs out of a low red car and stride up the entrance steps. The woman had a long-limbed, confident, hip-swaying walk that had made the skirt of her fabulous blue dress swirl. The blue bag tucked under her arm had a big gold clasp and her flimsy blue and gold sandals had heels even higher than the ones her mother wore when she was going somewhere important with Alexander. The woman hadn't bothered with the broken bell. She hadn't even bothered to knock. She'd just pushed open the big front door and stepped inside. After a while she'd returned to her car and taken out a bag and suitcases and what looked like a lot of dresses on hangers with plastic covers. She'd had to make three journeys to take in all of her things. That meant she was staying, probably for a long time.

While the black-haired woman was driving her car around the back, a youngish, fair-haired man had arrived. He'd carried a black bag and she guessed he was another doctor who'd come to see Alexander. And then there was an old woman, who'd started coming early in the morning and staying until the evening meal. Today she'd given Nathan a freshly baked loaf and a big bowl of lamb stew. He'd shared them with her, then she'd washed the dishes before setting off to spend the evening down here, in the quarry. There was no television in Nathan's bothy, just a big old radio his mother used to listen to. It didn't work any more. It was all a bit boring, and with so many people moving into the house it was going to be impossible to creep into Alexander's library to get one of the big books, or any other book to read.

The sun was setting. The quarry, with its deep pool of dark water, was filling with shadows. The rusty remains of the corrugated iron sheets that covered the saw house shut out what remained of the light, and it had become quite gloomy. Zarina crossed over to the edge of the raised floor and lowered herself down on to the rocky shelf she now regarded as her altar. She had to mark out the points of the compass before she took the paint back. She didn't have a compass, but Alexander had told her the rear of the house faced west, so the entrance side, the side that looked over the trees towards the quarry, must face east. Knowing that should enable her to mark her circle accurately enough. Symbols had to be drawn in the four quadrants, but she didn't know what they were; and she ought to draw a pentagon, but she couldn't remember whether it went inside the circle or enclosed it. She needed one of those books. She'd leave the compass points tonight, store the paint tin beside the remains of the huge engine that used to drive the saw and —

A sudden clatter of stones falling down the face of the quarry startled her. When they splashed into the pool the crows that nested high up on rocky ledges took flight and filled the air with a raucous cawing. Zarina pressed her slender body back against the plinth of the saw shed, stared up the high cliff and saw the figure of a man, silhouetted against the evening sky. He was striding around the rim of the quarry, along the narrow path that ran close to the edge, heading for the trees. She was sure it was the watcher, the man with the camera. He'd probably entered the grounds by climbing over the wall that bordered the Beckminster Road, perhaps at the place where they'd bricked up the old entrance to the quarry. The nurse who stayed for the night would be arriving soon. He'd probably come to watch her arrive and take more photographs.

3

The moans, the muttering, the strangled cries, were becoming louder. Samantha stepped away from the big Venetian window, with its view across the forecourt to the woodland that surrounded the Hall, and turned into the sunlit room. Alexander Meyer was lying on his back, his head and shoulders propped up by many pillows, his thin body reclining on two mattresses contained within the polished mahogany frame of an Empire-style bed. He was clearly in the grip of a terrible dream. Fear and anger were chasing one another across once handsome features; thin purple-tinged lips were trying to form words.

Marcus had been honest about the house. It was big and old; dilapidated, isolated, hidden in a wood. He'd been less than honest about the professor. Although he was obviously ill and very confused, his demise didn't seem imminent. That was fortunate; this was her second day here and so far she'd not been able to have any kind of a meaningful conversation with him.

She glanced at an elegant little French

clock on the bedside table. Almost 2.15 and the nurse who was scheduled to do the afternoon and evening shift hadn't arrived. The morning nurse had already left. She'd arranged to meet someone in Beckminster and Samantha had offered to stay with Alexander until her replacement came on duty.

Yesterday she'd explored most of the rooms, the grounds near the house, the warren of stables and outhouses at the back. Apart from making regular radiophone calls to the three men guarding the gates and patrolling the grounds, there were few demands on her time.

One of the nurses had told her Alexander's periods of clarity came and went. It was all to do with the opiates he'd been prescribed. They controlled his pain, but they made him confused and prone to strange and lurid dreams. When she had a chance, she'd talk to the doctor about reducing the dose before the illness progressed and his pain became less bearable. She didn't have an endless amount of time to strike up a rapport with the old man.

Samantha gazed down at his troubled face. His eyes were shifting from side to side beneath the lids; perspiration beaded his brow and glistened on pallid cheeks. She rounded the bed, took a towel and a box of alcohol-soaked tissues from the nurses' trolley and wiped his face and neck. Little moans of pleasure rustled in his throat. 'Rasha, Rasha,' he murmured, then eyes that were dazed and sightless fluttered open. When they eventually focused on her, his expression changed to one of pure terror.

'It's you, it really is you!' With a shaking hand he pushed the towel aside and tried to struggle up from the pillows.

Samantha smiled down at him, waiting for him to explain.

'Where's the other one?' he demanded, then turned his head and stared towards the misty net curtains. They were billowing into the room, floating on a faint breeze wafting in through the open window.

'Which other one?' Samantha whispered. She began to dab his brow with the towel again.

'The temple woman; there was another one, just like you, piercing eyes and a heavy black wig with a deep fringe. I think she was a priestess.'

'There's no one else here, Professor, and my hair's real, not a wig. I'm called Georgina; Georgina Grey. Marcus sent me.'

'The priest from the temple sent you; the priest who wears the jackal-headed mask. I heard him tell you to take me to The House of Purification.'

'You're in your bedroom, Professor — your bedroom at Sourbeck Hall.'

The net curtains billowed into the room.

He rolled his head on the pillows and stared, wide-eyed, at the misty whiteness. 'I'm in a mortuary tent.' Terror was making his voice shrill. He glanced at the nurses' metal trolley with its bright metal bowls and bottles, its packets of sterile things. 'You've taken me to the West Bank, to the place of the embalmers with their jars and hooks and knives.' He gazed up at Samantha, his mouth anguished, his eyes wide with fear. Suddenly, he arched his back and veins and sinews stood out like thick cords on his scrawny neck as he screamed, 'No, Rasha! Don't let him defile you. Don't let him touch you.' Then he collapsed back on the pillows, his chest heaving.

Samantha held him by the shoulders. 'You're dreaming, Professor.' She shook him gently. 'I'm Georgina, not a priestess. Anubis didn't send me. Your friend, Marcus, asked me to come to you.'

Confused grey eyes frowned up at her while she dabbed his brow with the towel. His face crumpled. 'Rasha's been summoned by Pharaoh Amenhotop,' he sobbed. 'He's besotted with her. She dances for him, and afterwards he fondles her breasts and thighs.

And he's so brazen. He takes these liberties while I'm there, while I'm watching.'

'Wake up, Professor.' Samantha shook his shoulders again. 'It's a dream, only a dream.' Despairing tears were coursing down his cheeks.

'And she delights in it,' he rambled on. 'His caresses give her pleasure. She melts at his touch, she told me so. Told me I had to stop behaving like a sulky boy and learn to accept it. Tonight they're going to lie together, on his couch, with the entire court looking on. Can a husband suffer any greater humiliation?'

Samantha picked up the towel, crossed the faded Turkish carpet and stepped into a tiny bathroom that had been formed in what had once been a linen store. She soaked the towel in cold water, returned to the bed and began to dab his face and shoulders and chest. 'You're having a dream, Professor. A terrible dream, but that's all it is: a terrible dream.'

The sudden cold made him shiver. Still frowning up at her, he demanded, 'Who are you?'

She repeated the name on her identity documents: 'Georgina; Georgina Grey. Your friend Marcus Soames, the major, sent me to watch over you. And you were having a bad dream.'

'Dream?' He shivered again. She began to

rub him briskly with a dry towel. 'So I was,' he mumbled tearfully. 'I have such dreadful dreams, so vividly real, so vile, populated by priests and kings and gods that are half man and half beast. Ancient Egypt. It's a part of me, it's in my blood; spent my life studying it, writing about it, exploring tombs and temples, translating scrolls and inscriptions.' He began to weep again. 'And in my dreams Rasha's always warm and beautiful, radiant with life, while I'm cold and unwashed and newly dead; being rowed across the Nile to the place where embalmers ply their noxious trade. And I'm filled with fear because I've forgotten the Words of Denial — when Anubis presents me to Osiris I'll not be able to make the negative confession. I'll be condemned to drift for ever in a dark and dreadful desolation.'

He fell silent while Samantha finished drying him, then whimpered, 'Rasha's left me, you see, without even leaving a note, and she's taken all the children with her. And I miss her. I miss her terribly.' He sighed and shook his head, as if trying to dispel the dream and his loss from his mind, then said, 'Where's Caroline?'

'She left, half an hour ago. We're waiting for Josie. Something must have delayed her.'

'Who did you say you were?'

'Georgina; Georgina Grey. Your old friend, Marcus, sent me.'

Understanding finally illuminated his face. 'I remember now. A few days ago. He came to see me. I was in a bit of a mess. He arranged a housekeeper and the nurses, and he promised to send me someone to keep me safe, someone special.' He frowned up at her. 'I thought it would be a man.'

She sat down beside him on the bed. 'Would you have preferred a man?'

'Good heavens, no. But for a while back there I was convinced you were a temple woman, a priestess perhaps.' He studied her intently. 'Not surprising, really: the black hair, the deep fringe, the crimson mouth.' His gaze lingered on the bodice of her dress, then lowered to the skirt, 'And the finely pleated linen.' He glanced up and gave her a libidinous smile. 'But I should have known; if you'd been a priestess your breasts would have been uncovered.'

The nurse had warned her that the morphine released him from his inhibitions, that he was prone to ask intimate questions and say inappropriate things. Samantha gave him a naughty-naughty look. 'You're fibbing, Professor. You know better than anyone that temple women, especially priestesses, were always fully clothed. It was only the musicians and dancing girls who bared their breasts.'

He let out a tired sigh. 'Damn. You've caught me out. And you're quite right, Georgina. May I call you Georgina, or should I call you Miss Grey?'

'I'd much prefer Georgina.'

Suddenly brightening, he said. 'You have a knowledge of Ancient Egypt? You understand the culture?'

'No more than most people, Professor. But I have spent almost two days in the library, waiting for you to wake up and talk to me. I've been reading your monographs, your translation of the *Book of the Dead*.' She smiled. 'You won't be found wanting when Anubis comes.'

'Can't remember a thing. Mind's like cotton wool.'

'Not even the Litany of Denial?'

He sighed. 'Not even that.'

Reaching out, she took his hand and recited, 'When we're presented to Osiris we should remember the Negative Confession: the things we must deny.' She tried to recall a text for him, any text, that she'd read in one of his books. Eventually she whispered softly, 'I am Yesterday and Tomorrow. I have the power to be born again. I am the divine hidden Soul, the father of the gods; the Lord who comes forth out of darkness.'

A smile that was almost seraphic illuminated his long, ascetic face. 'Nebseni, the Lord of Reverence: *Coming Forth by Day in the Underworld*: that I do remember.'

'You should: it's your translation.'

'And you can recite it all?'

'Some of it. I'm cursed with a photographic memory.'

'Surely a blessing, not a curse.'

'That depends on the things one keeps remembering.'

His gaze left her face and wandered over her oatmeal-coloured dress. Its high waist was tightly gathered beneath a low-cut bodice; the pleated skirt was full, the linen fine, almost filmy. He sighed. 'I do believe I've already encountered you in my dreams, Georgina.' Exhausted now, he relaxed back on the pillows, coughed, and swallowed with some difficulty.

'You seem thirsty. Would you like me to fetch you a drink?'

He nodded.

'Tea?'

He opened an eye and squinted up at her. 'Whisky.' An impish smile shaped his lips.

'Do the nurses allow you to have whisky?'

Both eyes flicked open. 'But of course.'

Samantha stroked his cheek. 'You're telling fibs again, Professor. They'd never let you have whisky.'

'It can be our secret.'

Deciding to make some use of the conversation, she whispered huskily, 'And are you going to share your other secrets with me?'

He chortled. 'I knew that was why Marcus sent you.'

'He sent me to protect you.'

'But only until I'd told you the things he wanted to know.'

'I'll keep you safe until you're well again.'

'I'll never be well again, Georgina. Anubis is waiting.' He closed his eyes and rambled on in Arabic, more to himself than to her: 'And he's becoming impatient. When evening comes and the light fades, I can see his great jackal-head grinning at me out of the shadows.'

'Then let him wait. We'll keep him hanging on so long he'll grow tired and slink away.'

'Aha! You speak Arabic?'

Samantha nodded.

'Another reason why Marcus sent you.'

She smiled, picked up her bag and slid the strap over her shoulder. 'I'll fetch your whisky.' As she moved past the window a sudden breeze tugged at the hem of her skirt and made the net curtains billow.

'Bottle's in the cabinet in the library, the one near the desk,' he called after her. 'And there's usually ice and ginger beer in the fridge in the kitchen. Bring two glasses. I'd rather not drink alone.'

Her stiletto heels thudded softly over the landing and down the stairs, then tap-tapped across the marble floor of the hall. The sound whispered around the coffered ceiling, echoed along passageways. She found the half-full bottle of whisky in the library, then headed back, crossed the hall and walked on down a gloomy corridor. She pushed at a green baize door. Bricks with a dark-green glaze formed a shoulder-high dado around the big kitchen; above it, white glazed bricks, most of them crazed, rose up to a ceiling dotted with hooks and crossed by ropes that raised and lowered long racks for drying washing. Tiny flakes of ancient whitewash, suspended in spiders' webs, were waiting to fall.

Norma Binnington, the grey-haired woman who came from the village to cook and keep house, was sliding a casserole dish into the Aga cooker. She slammed the door then glanced round at Samantha. 'Will the nurse who comes in the mornings be staying on for dinner?'

'Caroline? She left after she'd finished her shift. She's meeting someone in town.'

'But the one called Josie: she'll be here?'

'I hope so.' Samantha tugged open the fridge door, dislodged a tray of ice cubes from the freezer compartment and lifted a bottle of ginger beer from a rack. 'Do you have something I could put the ice in?'

Norma took a dish from an old Welsh dresser and passed it over.

'She's late,' Samantha said. 'I'm just getting the professor a drink.'

'I used to work for his father when I was a girl.' Norma settled her broad posterior on the edge of the table. She seemed to want to talk. 'Came here straight from school. Used to help the cook. House wasn't all that much better then. Be glad when I'm going home tonight. Don't really care for the place; too many dark corners and empty rooms. And there's no one to keep me company down here. Scares me a bit. And I keep thinkin' I hear things.'

'Hear things?' Samantha took a couple of glasses from the dresser and put them, with the dish of ice cubes and the bottles, on a tray.

'Footsteps in the yard at the back. Sometimes I see people out there.'

'What kind of people?'

'Once it was a man. Foreign-looking, swarthy, wearing one of those bomber jacket things. And I've seen a child: a girl with long curly hair. Dirty-looking, dark-skinned, bit like a gypsy. Can't be sure, though. Don't wear my glasses in the house, and the back yard never catches the sun and it's gloomy inside all those doorways and openings. Trouble is, when you're shut up in this old place all day you can start imagining things. Perhaps it was a couple of gypsies, poking around, trying to find something to steal.'

Samantha picked up the tray. 'When the nurse arrives I'll come and keep you company. I've got papers to go through, but I can do that just as well in here as in the library.'

She pushed through the green baize door and headed back down the dark corridor that led to the hall. When she reached the foot of the stairs she heard voices drifting down from the professor's room. She stood and listened, but couldn't make out the words, just the professor's thin, breathless voice and the deeper, stronger voice of another man.

Alarm quickened her pulse. She stepped out of her shoes and began to climb. When she reached the first landing, she placed the tray on the sill of a tall stained-glass window, then kept close to the wall so the stairs wouldn't creak as she wound her way upwards. She slid her hand inside her bag, gripped the butt of her gun, then crept across the upper landing and peered around the edge of the half-open bedroom door.

A stocky, dark-haired man, wearing a half-sleeved white jacket, was holding an ampoule up to the light while he drew the contents into a hypodermic syringe.

The professor, his upper arm exposed, was eying him warily. 'Where's Josie?'

The man withdrew the syringe and dropped the empty ampoule into the top pocket of his jacket. He began to wipe the professor's arm with cotton wool. 'Josie?'

'Nurse Stockwell. I hope she's not ill.'

'Don't think so. I got a call to come over here. They said she'd gone into Beckminster; probably got delayed there.' He tossed the wad of cotton wool on to the trolley and lowered the syringe.

Samantha heaved at the door, heard it crash against the wall. 'Take the needle away from his arm.' She stepped into the room and stood, arms outstretched, the gun grasped in both hands.

The man glanced up, his thumb still on the plunger.

'Take it away. Now!' she snarled

'Who — '

'Don't even think about it. Just do as I say. Get the needle away from his arm, and step clear of the bed.'

'Are you mad? I'm a nurse. I've been — '

'Take the needle away from his arm and get clear of the bed.' Anger exploded in her voice. 'Do it now, or I'll kill you.'

He stepped back. 'You're making a fool of yourself. When I return to the agency I'll — '

'Put the syringe on the trolley and come round to the foot of the bed.'

Slowly, sullenly, nervous eyes locked on hers, he did as she asked. He seemed to be trying to assess her resolve, her willingness to use the gun.

'Get down on your knees.' She gestured with the gun. 'Just there. And face the far wall.'

'Why should I do this? You're insane. I'm a replacement nurse, sent to attend a patient. You can check my papers; you can call the people at the agency.'

'I told you to get down on your knees and face the far wall. If you don't do it, I'll kill you.'

'And I told you I am a nurse attending — '

Green eyes glittered. 'Do it now!' She tugged at the breech and let it clatter back on its spring. 'Do it or die.'

He dropped to his knees. She stepped up behind him and swung the heavy gun down on the side of his head. He groaned. She delivered another blow, then put her foot in his back and forced him, face down, on to the carpet. She groped in her bag, found handcuffs, circled one of his wrists with bright metal and clicked the ratchet home. While he was still dazed she captured the other, then slid her fingers into the pocket of his jacket and took out the tiny glass cylinder. Numbers and letters were etched on its side, but nothing to tell her what it had contained. She rose to her feet. 'What was in the syringe?'

He muttered into the carpet. She swung a kick between his parted legs, felt the pointed toe of her shoe sink into soft tissue. A sudden intake of breath was followed by an agonized scream.

'I shan't ask you again. What was in the syringe?'

'Diamorphine.'

'Tell me the truth, or you'll never see Egypt again.'

'I don't want to see Egypt. I'm British; born in Coventry. I'm a nurse. I work for an agency.' His voice rose to an angry scream. 'And you're in big trouble, you crazy woman. You can't — '

'You're lying. You're Egyptian. You've lived in the south, most of your life, probably near Luxor. I can hear the dialect, even when you're speaking English.'

'I'm British, British, British,' he screamed. 'I've never been to Egypt. I'm a nurse. I'm — '

'In pain,' she interrupted, feigning sympathy. 'And we both know the best thing for severe pain, don't we?' She paused, he didn't answer, so she went on. 'Diamorphine's the best thing for pain.' She stepped over to the trolley, took the syringe from the bowl, then knelt beside him and pressed the needle against his neck. 'You need this, don't you? You need it badly. Thirty seconds and the pain will start to fade; a minute and you'll — '

'No!' The word came out as a scream. 'No, in the name of God, no.'

'You don't want me to soothe the pain?' She pressed the needle harder. His body became rigid as he strained to avoid the prick of the hypodermic.

'Please,' he whimpered. 'Please.'

'Please what? Please give it to me?'

'No, I don't want it.' He began to sob. 'Take it away. Please, take it away.'

Samantha rose to her feet and dropped the syringe back into the metal bowl. 'Get up.'

Slowly, painfully, he shuffled his knees under his body, his rump rose in the air, then he lurched to his feet and staggered back against the bed. She grabbed his arm, steadied him, then went to the professor and drew his pyjama jacket over his shoulders. 'Are you okay?' She began to button it up.

'I'm fine.' He gave her a shocked little smile. 'I'm absolutely fine.' His eyes were brighter and he was more alert, more alive. The excitement seemed to have given him some energy.

'I left the whisky on the stairs,' she said. 'I'll get one of the guards to bring it up. He'll sit with you while I take our friend somewhere and persuade him to tell me what he's done with Nurse Stockwell.'

* * *

Zarina gazed up at the sloping ceiling. She was bored. There were no books or magazines in Nathan's pokey little cottage, and no television. And she desperately wanted to go to Alexander's library, take at least one of the grimoires and find paper and a pencil so she could copy out the spells.

She might never get into the house now. The place seemed to get busier and busier. Yesterday, she'd knelt on the bed and watched the black-haired woman through the tiny attic window. She'd been inspecting the stables and outhouses that enclosed the rear yard. The woman usually wore dresses and high-heeled shoes, but yesterday she'd worn tight black trousers, a crimson Cossack-style blouse and black lace-up boots. Zarina guessed there was something heavy in her bag because it pulled the shoulder strap very tight.

The woman had stood for quite a while in the shadowy interior of one of the stables, watching as Nathan balanced his mirror on the spout of the pump and had his early-morning wash and shave at the old horse trough. She must have known he was deaf, because when she eventually walked over she made sure he could see her. She'd held out her hand and said, 'I'm Georgina, and I think you must be Nathan.' She had a soft, husky voice and she'd spoken slowly, to make sure Nathan could read her lips. Her lips were very red. They gleamed like freshly spilled blood.

He'd been too shy to take her hand, so she'd passed him the towel and held his shaving mug while he dried himself.

Red mouth, red blouse, red fingernails: the woman seemed to like red. And she always wore mascara and eye shadow, just like her mother when she was going out with Alexander, but nowhere near as much as her mother.

Nathan didn't scare her like he did most people. People, especially women, usually shuddered when they first saw him. Then they tried not to look at him. With those huge shoulders and muscular arms and thick, stumpy legs he was a bit like the ogre in the book of fairy tales Alexander had given her when she was small. Foxy-red hair sprouted out of his ears, smothered the backs of his arms and hands, made his eyebrows incredibly spiky. Even his mouth, fleshy and loose and filled with wide-spaced stumpy teeth, was a bit like the giant's in the picture book. Nathan wasn't a giant, of course; he was just big-chested and immensely strong.

Nathan liked the Georgina woman. She could tell by the way he grinned and snuffled and became shy when she came up to him. Zarina suspected she was trying to put him under a spell; like her mother did with Alexander when she wanted to wheedle something out of him. Her mother always got what she wanted. Alexander would give her anything. Women's spells were very powerful.

Yesterday evening, when Nathan had gone to the kitchen door to collect their dinner, the black-haired woman had answered. She'd tried to coax him inside to eat with her and the nurses, but he wouldn't go in. He couldn't; he shared what they gave him with her, so he just kept on shaking his head and holding out his bowl. Eventually, the woman had laughed, then she'd taken his bowl inside and filled it with some meaty stew, and given him a dish of peas and new potatoes, a fresh loaf, a pat of butter, some apples and four bottles of beer in a basket. She was much kinder than the housekeeper who came from the village. There'd been heaps for them to share, and Nathan had poured a little beer into a cup for her. She'd hated the bitter taste of it.

Someone was shouting and cursing in Arabic. The sound was growing louder. Zarina leaped up, knelt on the bed beside the grimy attic window and looked down into the yard. A man staggered out of the scullery passage. His arms were tied behind his back and blood was running down the side of his face and dripping on his white jacket. She opened the window a little so she could hear better and put her face close to the glass. The black-haired woman followed him out. She was holding a big black gun and jabbing him in the back with it. 'Get over there.' Her voice was hoarse and angry. 'Go through that door.' They disappeared into a storeroom and the door crashed shut behind them.

Seconds later she heard screams — a man's, not a woman's — and he was yelling, 'Whore, whore, you filthy whore. You don't deserve the name of woman.'

Then she heard the woman saying, 'Where is she? Where's the nurse? Tell me.' The sound of sickening blows reached her attic window, each one punctuated by the words, 'Tell me, tell me, tell me.' And then, 'If you don't tell me, I'll damage you. You won't be a man any more. I'll inflict pain more intense than you could possibly imagine.'

'A kilometre down the Beckminster Road, just beyond the Milton crossroads.' The man was sobbing now. 'There's a gateway into a wood. She's in there, in the boot of a car, a black Daimler. About fifty metres in from the road.'

The woman emerged from the storeroom. Blood was splattered over the bodice and skirt of her dress. She slammed the heavy door shut just as two of the men in baggy blue uniforms came running into the yard. She heard one of them saying, 'Sorry, ma'am. The nurse's car came through the gate pretty fast. The driver looked like a blonde woman, so we didn't wave it down.'

'He's in there. Don't go in. You must be able to say you never saw him. One of you stand outside until I get back, the other go into the house and up to the professor's room.' She began to climb into a low red car parked just inside one of the stables. 'There's a bottle of whisky on the stairs. Take it up and give him as much as he wants — and stay with him.'

The engine roared into life and the car snarled out of the yard. Zarina listened to it circling the house and crossing the forecourt, then the sound faded to a distant rumble as it sped off down the long driveway.

One of the men positioned himself with his back to the storeroom door, his gun cradled in his arm; the other dashed into the scullery passage. Zarina let out her breath. She was tingling with excitement. The feeling of boredom had been dispelled. Something new seemed to be happening every day. Suddenly overwhelmed by an urge to go to the lavatory, she rolled off the bed, climbed down the rickety ladder to the landing and then down a flight of narrow stairs to the living room. Nathan's tiny back yard was hidden behind the stable block. Zarina scampered across it and locked herself in the whitewashed place where the smell of disinfectant was so strong it made her eyes water.

* * *

Samantha swept over the crest of a rise then braked hard when she saw the road snaking steeply downwards. Tyres squealed as she manoeuvred around the first bend. When she rounded the second she could see the crossroads at the bottom of the hill and the wood the man had mentioned, rising up the distant slope like a dark scar. She plunged on down, swept through the crossroads and surged up the far side of the valley. An opening in an old stone wall loomed then flashed past. She slowed the car and cruised at a sedate pace for another hundred yards before pulling into a lay-by.

She ran back along the overgrown verge, her bag bouncing against her hip, the long grass dragging at her skirt. The wood was casting a dark shadow over the road. Old, abandoned to nature, the high branches of its ancient trees reached out over the carriageway; lower down, the vegetation had been trimmed back to give the sparse traffic an unobstructed passage along the road. The opening in the wall led to an overgrown track that curved into the trees. The men had planned the abduction well. Isolated, hidden, it was a perfect place to conceal the nurse until their business at the Hall was over.

Shadows deepened as she advanced into the wood. After fifty paces she began to move more stealthily, keeping her face and blood-stained dress below the line of the bracken that covered the banks on either side of the track.

Bracken gave way to coarse grass. Up ahead, shafts of sunlight slanting down into a small clearing gleamed on the coachwork of a black Daimler. The car had been reversed, made ready to be driven back down the track to the road. A diplomatic badge was fixed to the radiator grille, and *Republic of Egypt* was emblazoned on a panel above the licence plate. The dark hair of a man was just visible above the roof. Smoke was curling upwards; he was enjoying a cigarette. Samantha edged closer.

The forest was too tangled and overgrown for her to circle the clearing through the trees, so she had to approach along the side of the car. When she rounded the boot she saw he was leaning back, elbows on the lid, his outstretched legs crossed, gazing up at bright patches of sky. In profile his face was exceptionally handsome: nose straight, mouth and chin firm, his faintly pockmarked cheeks roughened by stubble. His dark suit and black shoes looked handmade and expensive.

Quite close to him now, she gripped the heavy automatic in both hands and raised her outstretched arms. He remained oblivious to her; perhaps the tedium of waiting had made him less alert. Samantha watched him draw on his cigarette and inhale deeply, then whispered, 'Just stay where you are. Don't move.'

He jerked upright and glanced around. When he saw her standing in the dappled sunlight, he coughed out a cloud of smoke.

'I said, don't move. If you move, I'll kill you.'

'Who the hell are you? Put the gun down. What do you think you're doing? Look at the badge and plates on the car. Don't you know — '

'Where's the nurse?'

'What nurse? I've no idea who you're talking about. I'm an attaché at the embassy. I was taking a break from driving. You can't — '

A frenzied banging erupted inside the boot.

Samantha nodded towards the car. 'Unfasten it, let the lid rise, then stand back, but not too far back, just a couple of paces.'

His mouth curved in a sneer. He'd recovered from his shock and his stare had become contemptuous. Tall, strong, imbued with a male arrogance that had been nurtured by culture, he was going to be difficult.

'I said open the boot and stand back.'

'Come over here, you idle bitch, and open it yourself.'

She squeezed the trigger, felt the recoil up her outstretched arms, winced at the deafening roar as she sent a bullet winging past his ear.

He flinched. His body tensed. Shock, surprise, a sudden fear, had chased away the swagger. Now his jittery eyes were darting this way and that, assessing the situation, checking to see if she was alone.

'I won't ask you again. Get the boot open and step back. Make any sudden moves and the next shot's going to kill you.'

He pressed his thumb against the catch and the lid rose. Samantha waved the gun, directing him to move away. After two backward steps, she snapped, 'That's far enough.'

Josie's tousled blonde head appeared over the rim of the voluminous boot. A wide band of silvery adhesive tape had been stretched over her mouth; the front of her dress torn open. Her arms were tied behind her back. When she tried to swing a leg over the sill she failed and rolled back.

Samantha noted the half-exposed breasts and laddered tights. When her gaze flashed back to the man, her eyes glittered. 'Get that stupid sneer off your face,' she hissed, 'and listen to me carefully because your life's going to depend on your doing exactly — '

'Are you blind? Are you deaf? I have diplomatic immunity, and I object to the threatening way you're treating me. I demand that you call your superiors.'

'I don't have any superiors. Listen to me — ' He opened his mouth to speak again.

'I said listen to me,' she snapped. 'This is a powerful weapon. If a bullet from it hits you, no matter where it hits you, you won't get up again. They expand and shred as they pass through flesh and tear it away. Even if you survive the trauma, the wounds won't heal and they can't be repaired. Do you understand that?'

He nodded.

'So, you're going to do as I say?'

He glared at her for a long moment, then nodded again. Loathing and anger were smouldering in dark eyes that seemed too large, a little too feminine, for a man; sweat gleamed on his brow and pock-marked cheeks.

'Put your hands behind your head and walk slowly towards that fallen tree at the edge of the clearing.' She gestured with the gun.

He did as she asked. She followed him at a distance.

The gnarled trunk was massive, chest high, and vegetation had grown up between what remained of its branches. Beyond the sunlit clearing, its tangled roots clawed their way into the darkness.

'Turn round and face me, then remove your clothes. Start with the shoes.'

'You want me to undress?' His disbelieving

voice was outraged.

'Undress, strip, take your clothes off — what part of that don't you understand? Put the things in a neat pile.'

He lowered his gaze to the blood-splattered bodice and skirt of her dress. 'Have you killed Ibrahim?'

'Just a few little cuts and bruises, that's all.' Her tone hardened. 'I'm losing patience,' she snapped angrily. 'If you don't . . . '

He crouched down, unlaced his shoes and pulled them off, then rose, removed his jacket and unfastened his tie. Eyes, brimming with hatred, were holding her in an unblinking stare. Tense and watchful, she stared back at him down the barrel of the gun.

He unfastened gold cufflinks, unbuttoned his shirt, peeled it over his shoulders and dropped it on the pile; then he unzipped his trousers and stepped out of them when they fell.

'And the socks.'

Hopping, first on one leg, then the other, he tugged them off.

She jerked the gun. 'And your underpants.'

He hooked his thumbs under the waistband. 'Do you enjoy this?' he snarled. 'Do you take pleasure in humiliating me?' He pushed them down and kicked them towards the pile.

'Did you and your friend enjoy humiliating the nurse? Stand up straight and put your hands behind your head.'

Crimson mouth contemptuous, she slowly swept her gaze down the dark torso. His body was completely hairless: hard, muscular, well cared for. She studied his sullen face. The pock-marks, the dark stubble, were the imperfections needed to transform a large-eyed pretty boy into a handsome man. Suddenly noticing what she thought was a tattoo, she snapped, 'Turn until I can see your left side. And keep your hands behind your head.'

He turned. She could see it clearly now, a letter and number sequence tattooed on his chest, just beneath his right armpit. 'How long were you in Abu Zaabal prison?'

'Two years.'

'You were a political prisoner?'

'I plotted against the old regime.' He paused for a moment, then added, 'Along with others, I was freed by revolutionaries after they fought an hour-long battle with the guards.'

'And now you serve the new regime. What's your name?'

'Aman. Aman al-Nafiri.' Fear had finally surfaced through the anger in his voice; a muscle was twitching in his thigh. Decaying leaves rustled and small twigs snapped as he slowly shuffled round to face her again. His whole body seemed tense, poised for sudden movement, and his dark eyes were darting this way and that, frantically searching for some means of saving himself.

'I think your crimes embraced more than insurrection, Aman.' She tightened her grip on the gun and continued to hold him in an unblinking stare. For it to fully achieve its purpose, the bullet had to enter at the back of his head, but would he obey a command to turn his back towards her? If she asked him to do that, he might sense he was about to be killed. Desperation would make him reckless. The killing would become chaotic and messy, possibly dangerous. She had to give him hope.

Keeping her voice calm, she said, 'I want you to remain where you are until we've driven away, then you can dress and wait for your friend to return with the car.' She watched the tension drain from his body, his jittery eyes stop wandering, then went on: 'The nurse won't want you staring at her when she climbs out of the boot, and I find your body repulsive, so I'd like you to turn your back towards us. Do you understand me?'

He nodded.

'Then do it.'

He turned, slid his hands from behind his head and rested them on the trunk of the fallen tree.

'I'll be watching you. Don't make any stupid moves.' Samantha held her breath and squeezed the trigger. His body jerked. Blood, bone and brains splattered over rough bark, then he slumped down on the decaying leaves.

She ran back to the car. The nurse was lying on her side, propped up on an elbow, watching her approach over the rim of the boot. Samantha peeled the tape from her mouth. 'Did they hurt you? Did they — '

'They mauled me, put their filthy groping hands everywhere. And all the time they were sneering at me, talking in Arabic, calling me a kafir whore. They thought I couldn't understand, but I know enough of the language to know what they were saying.'

Samantha reached for Josie's wrists. They'd been secured with a cable tie. She laid the gun in the boot, searched amongst the clutter in her bag, found a knife and began to saw at the tough plastic. 'And what were they saying?'

The nurse was shaking now. She was close to tears. 'That I was too good to waste; that when they'd got their business over with they'd use me until they were exhausted, then they'd kill me. When the other one left for the house he made this one promise he wouldn't start anything until he got back.'

The cable tie parted. Samantha took the woman's hands and began to massage her wrists.

'I was scared,' Josie sobbed. 'I've never been so scared. I was so scared I peed myself. I just couldn't help it.' She swung her legs out of the boot and Samantha helped her down. After the nurse had straightened her skirt, she turned and drew it tight. 'Does anything show?'

'No. There's nothing; absolutely nothing. Will you be okay if I leave you for a moment? I've got to deal with the body.'

Josie nodded. 'Do you need any help? I could — '

'You've had enough. I can manage, and you wouldn't want to see what's left of his face.' Samantha led her round to the front of the car, sat her in the passenger seat and left her, weeping and hugging herself. She recovered her gun from the boot, then returned to the fallen tree and rolled Aman onto his back. The emerging shell had torn away the brow and eyes, the nose and most of the cheeks. The lower jaw remained, hanging loose at the base of an almost empty skull.

She searched amongst the undergrowth,

found a suitable branch and used it to scrape away the drift of mouldering leaves. When she'd cleared a space, she rolled the body into it, took the gun from her bag and loosed a shot to destroy what was left of his jaws and teeth. Then she raised his right arm and fired another round to blast away the strip of tattooed flesh. Short of hacking off his hands, something she baulked at, it was as much as she could do to conceal the man's identity.

She picked up the branch again, used it to push the body beneath the tree and rake leaves over it, then gathered up the man's clothes and headed for the car.

Josie Stockwell's face was pale and blotchy, but she'd stopped crying. Frozen with shock now, she seemed unnaturally calm and composed. They gazed at one another in silence for a while, then the nurse asked, 'Did you kill the other one, the one who came to the house?'

'Not yet, but I will later, after I've questioned him. I should have questioned this one, but he'd have made a dangerous captive and I didn't want to linger here.' She studied the nurse for a moment longer, then decided to voice her concerns. 'You are in the Service? You've had security clearance?'

'I am and I have. Full clearance.'

Reassured, Samantha went on, 'This hasn't

happened. You haven't seen anything. You don't know anything. When we part, it must be as if we'd never met.'

The woman nodded. 'Of course. I understand.'

'Your life, and my life, depend on silence.'

Josie nodded again. 'I just want to forget it. The last thing I want to do is talk about it. And I daren't tell my husband. He'd go crazy.'

The keys were in the ignition. Samantha started the car. 'I'm parked in a lay-by up the hill. If I take us there, could you drive this thing back to the Hall?'

'I think so. The roads are pretty deserted around here.' Suddenly remembering, Josie said, 'We'd better get back. The professor won't have been cleaned and changed, and he needs his medication.'

'I left him with one of the guards and a bottle of whisky. It was the best I could do.' They began to bounce down the overgrown track, bushes and bracken chafing against the sides of the car.

'Thank God you came,' Josie said. 'If you hadn't I'd probably be dead now.' She turned and looked at Samantha. 'Marcus must have been expecting trouble; why else would he have sent you? He told me it would be a pleasant change from office routine, a brief return to nursing, I could practice my old skills in a big house in the countryside — almost as good as a holiday.'

Samantha began to laugh. 'He's an outrageous old charmer. He'd sweet talk you into anything.' Changing the subject, she asked, 'How did the men persuade you to stop?'

'They'd driven their car on to the verge. One of them was lying in the road, close to an old bike, and the other was kneeling beside him. When he saw me coming he stood up and flagged me down. It was an expensive car, he was well dressed; I didn't even think about it. I just pulled up and ran over. They grabbed me, put the tape over my mouth and threw me in the boot. After they'd both mauled me, the tall one took me to the wood.'

They emerged from the track, bounced out on to the road and headed up the hill.

Josie said, 'I don't know whether I can make the journey from the base to the house any more. I think I'll be too scared.'

'Perhaps you should all move into the Hall; live there to avoid the travelling.'

'Caroline and Nicole won't like that. There are some nice blokes on the base and they hold dances in the mess on Saturday nights.'

'Dances don't appeal to you?'

'I think I told you, I have a husband. He's in the Royal Navy, a submariner. He's halfway through a six-month tour.'

Samantha parked behind her Ferrari in the lay-by. The nurse was gazing at her with curious eyes.

'Why do you expose yourself to such danger?' she asked softly. 'Why do you kill for them?'

Samantha stared out through the windscreen, at the overgrown hedgerows and the narrow country road, shimmering in the afternoon heat. Eventually she said, 'My husband was murdered by a terrorist. He was a doctor; killed by a sniper while he was attending a patient on a kibbutz near the Gaza strip. We'd been married for six months. And terrorists murdered my half-sister and her husband and their little girl. So I could say it's a craving for revenge, but it's a lot more complicated than that.' She collected her thoughts, then went on. 'The killing haunts me. I dream about it, see the faces of the men I've killed. Angry faces, terrified faces; old, young, dark-skinned, white-skinned, bearded, clean-shaven. I see the light fading from their eyes, the anger and terror draining from their faces as they drift into death.' Her voice fell to a husky whisper. 'And when it really starts to trouble me, when the enormity of it overwhelms me and I'm sickened to my soul, I think of my husband. I remember what they took from me, and the pain, the sense of loss, obliterate all the anguish, all the guilt.'

She'd said enough. Close to tears herself now, she pushed open the door and stepped out of the car. 'Slide behind the wheel. It's an automatic. You're okay with an automatic?'

Josie nodded and began to clamber across the car.

'I'll follow you in my car so I can watch for trouble. I'll see you back at the Hall.'

4

The encrypted phone was noisy; faint clicks and bleeps continuously interrupted the normal background hiss. Samantha was sitting behind Alexander's desk in the mullioned bay that projected from the side of the library. She was gazing out over a sunlit orchard. Marcus's secretary had gone to fetch him from a meeting. The woman hadn't argued; she hadn't suggested she call back. The old schemer must have been expecting her to call. Perhaps he already knew about the incident yesterday, or perhaps he was hoping for a progress report. He certainly —

'That you, Sam?'

She swung the chair round to face the desk. 'It's me, Marcus. Phone's making funny noises this morning.'

'They've increased the level of encryption: algorithm changes every three seconds. They've not smoothed out the wrinkles yet. Has Alexander begun to talk?'

'I didn't have a proper conversation with him until yesterday. He's awash with morphine; comatose or sleeping most of the time. I'm going to ask the doctor to reduce the dose. I need him alert if I'm to find out what he knows.'

'The chief's becoming very edgy, Sam. The Americans have an interest in this and they're getting impatient, and our own people need the information. I was hoping — '

His urgings began to irritate her. 'There was an attempt on his life yesterday,' she broke in. 'Two men, Egyptian nationals, waylaid one of the nurses on her way to the house and bundled her into the boot of a car. One of them took her to a wood while the other came here. He wore a white jacket and blonde wig to get past the guards near the gateway.'

'Guards should have been more alert. They were hand-picked for the job, dammit.'

'They were way back from the opening, where they couldn't be seen, and it's gloomy under the trees near the start of the drive. I've had Nathan re-hang the gates and instructed the men to stop and question all visitors now.'

'Did he get to Alexander?'

'I found him in the bedroom, about to give him an injection. I've kept the syringe. You can have the contents checked, but I'm certain they're lethal.'

'And?'

'I dragged him off, put him under guard in a store round the back, then went to find the nurse.'

'She okay?'

'Serious sexual assault. She overheard them say they were going to kill her after they'd killed the professor.'

'They raped her?'

'If you define rape as penetration, no, but it was pretty dreadful. She's moved into the house — she can't face the car journey any more. The other nurses have decided to stay on at the base. They don't care for the isolation here.'

'And Alexander's okay?'

'He's fine. I think he found the diversion exciting.'

'What about the bodies?'

Samantha smiled. He'd assumed there'd be bodies. 'One's hidden under the trunk of a fallen tree in the wood. Before I killed him I made him take off his clothes. He had a tattoo, a letter and number sequence under his right arm; he admitted he'd spent time in Abu Zaabal prison. I removed the tattoo and destroyed his face and jaws. There are still his finger prints and DNA, but if they're not held on file it won't be easy to make an ID. Nathan buried the other one for me. He disposes of Alexander's incontinence pads in a trench in an old herb garden. I got him to deepen a section, bury the body under the bags and sprinkle it with quick lime.'

'Can we trust him?'

'He's deaf and dumb, acts like an imbecile and makes Quasimodo look like Michelangelo's *David*, but he's really quite smart and he's incredibly strong and capable. I'm sure I can trust him.'

'The one you caught in the bedroom, was he naked when he was buried?'

'Yes, I made him undress; it makes searching the clothing easier. I put a bag over what was left of his head to hide it from Nathan; tied a grain sack around his lower half.'

'And the car? What's happened to that?'

'It's in one of the stables. Embassy Daimler with a diplomatic badge and plates. I ran the scanner over it; no sign of a tracker. Searched it, but didn't find anything useful. Do you want me to dispose of it?'

'I'll have it collected. We'll bring it back here, take it apart, have a good look at it, then fix a tracker and a bug and park it near their embassy. I presume you got the men's names?'

'When I interrogated the one who managed to get into the house he told me his name was Ibrahim Zayan. That tallied with the name on his fake nursing agency ID card, so it could be false. The one who stayed with the nurse said he was called Aman al-Nafiri. That checked against the embassy accreditation papers he was carrying. The tattooed letter-number sequence was . . . ' she flicked over the page in a tiny notebook, 'AVD53920. I've bundled up their clothes and put wallets, watches, jewellery and papers in named envelopes. I'll hand them to the man who collects the car. What's he going to be called?'

'Mmm . . . Wordsworth, Lakeland Couriers.'

'We are being literary, Marcus. Tell him he's collecting from Shirley Temple.'

'Did you take photographs?'

'Only of Ibrahim. I'll copy it onto a memory stick and put it with the clothes. Too risky to take one of Aman. I could tell he was waiting for a chance to jump me before I killed him, and there was nothing useful to photograph after he'd died. When I questioned the one who'd pretended to be a nurse he said the new regime was arresting and torturing anyone and everyone known to have been involved in drug trafficking and corruption of any kind.' She flicked back through the notebook, 'He talked about a man called Naguib Masud and someone called Abdel Fouad. I mentioned the names to Alexander. He knew both men: one was a senior official in the Ministry of the Interior, the other a member of one of the Regional

Councils for Antiquities. More important, they knew a great deal about Alexander and his old contacts. That worried him.'

'Things could get difficult.'

'They already are difficult, Marcus. Have you considered moving Alexander out; hiding him somewhere more secure?'

'First thing I suggested to him, but he refused. He's determined to die in the family home, in the bed his father died in. You've got to beguile him, Sam. Make him fall in love with you, persuade him to tell you what he knows, then we'll pull you out.'

'He adores his wife, Marcus. He's desolate without her. He dreams about her. He's not going to be bewitched or beguiled.'

'He's a heterosexual male. If a pulse is still beating, you can enchant him. Be nice to him. Wear some of your fancy frocks.'

'I don't wear *fancy frocks*,' she retorted icily. 'I wear fashionable dresses.'

He was laughing softly. 'A fashionable dress, then. Something figure-hugging. Display some cleavage, show a bit of leg.'

'It's enough that I kill for you, Marcus. I'm not prepared to act the tart as well.'

'You don't mind your man-servant thinking you're a tart.'

'I've told you a hundred times, Marcus, he's not my man-servant; he's my dearest friend. And I leave him his illusions because if he knew how I earned money he'd be so disgusted he'd run a mile.' She steered the conversation into calmer waters. 'Have you had any luck tracing Alexander's wife?'

'There's no record of her or the children having left the country, but that doesn't mean she hasn't managed to get out. We only did a basic check. The chief's not prepared to allocate the resources to do any more.'

'Do you want me to make some inquiries; see if I can come up with anything?'

'I want you to discover everything Alexander knows; that's the important thing. Searching for his wife and children is quite secondary; it would be too much of a distraction.'

'You're very callous, Marcus. Deep down, I don't think you give a damn about the man.'

'I have a higher duty than any I owe to Alexander. And you're being well paid to get that information.'

Pompous old bore, Samantha fumed. He'd be reminding her he was related to royalty next: sixty-third, or was it ninety-ninth, in line to the throne? She said, 'It's as you thought, Marcus. He's sure that when he's told you all he knows you'll withdraw the nursing care and the protection.' She gave him a moment to reflect, then suggested, 'Why don't I do a deal with him? If I find his wife, he tells me everything. And let's face it, someone could be holding her against her will, hoping to use her to bring pressure on Alexander.'

'If that was the case, whoever had her would have made a move days ago. And you might make this arrangement and not find his wife, and even if you did he could renege on it.'

'Give me that little research team back. I could talk to Alexander about where she might have gone, consider tactics, and if there's anything worth following up the team could feed useful background information to me.'

'His wife and children aren't our concern,' Marcus insisted. 'I want you to stay close to Alexander, talk to him, find out what he knows. The men sent by the embassy failed to kill him. They want him silenced. It's only a matter of days before they try again.'

'I'm having the outside of the house constantly patrolled. When I leave it, I station a guard by the door to Alexander's room. He'd be no safer with me there. Give me the team back, Marcus. Let me see what I can make of it.'

'It's the time, Sam, and the mounting cost. The chief's becoming very concerned about the cost.'

'She's concerned because we don't have the information. If I can find his wife, if he's got her with him again, if he knows he's not alone, he'll feel more secure and begin to tell me what he knows. Give me the team back, Marcus.'

She heard an exasperated sigh. After a long silence, he said, 'You can have them for two weeks,' he sounded reluctant, resentful almost, 'then we'll review the situation. But try to keep calls to daylight hours; they'll be assigned to other operators through the night.'

'Marcus . . . ?'

'I'm still here.'

'Send six hundred rounds for a Heckler sub with the courier who comes to collect the car.'

Samantha clicked off the phone, swung the chair round and gazed out over the sunlit orchard. Nathan emerged from an outhouse carrying green plastic sacks. He strode off between the apple trees, his short and slightly bowed legs giving him a rolling gait; the red hair on his head and arms coarse and straight, like the pelt of a fox. He stopped, picked up a windfall, rubbed it on his check shirt, then bit into it before lurching on through an archway that led to the old herb garden.

A sound, barely audible, of a handle being turned, reached her down the high, book-lined room. The door creaked open, then the latch clicked as it closed. Samantha slid the battered automatic pistol from her bag and crept to the mouth of the bay. She peered along the line of glass-topped display cases. A girl of about eleven or twelve, wearing a grimy gingham blouse and dirty jeans, her dusky face half-hidden beneath a curtain of matted hair, was moving a library ladder along the rows of books. She settled it close to the door, just beneath the topmost shelf, then climbed it with a cat-like confidence. After studying the spines of some large, leather-bound volumes for a moment, she tried to slide one out. It was heavy, wedged between its neighbours, and she swayed on the ladder as she tried to tug it free.

Samantha laid her gun on the desk, stepped out of her shoes and, silent in her stockinged feet, crept towards the intruder. Positioning herself at the foot of the ladder, she gazed up at worn jeans stretched tight over the buttocks and hips of a child moving into puberty. The book suddenly slid free, the girl swayed back, almost dropped it, then regained her balance and began to descend. She stepped to the floor, turned to leave, then froze when she saw Samantha. Eyes wide and bright, like a startled hare's, she let out a frightened little gasp.

Samantha smiled down at her. It was obvious who the child was. The likeness to the photograph of her mother was incredibly strong. 'Zarina,' she murmured softly. Her smile widened. The girl darted towards the door. Samantha lunged forward, caught hold of her arm and drew her back. 'Don't dash away, Zarina. I'd like to talk to you. I'd like you to tell me where you've been.'

'You've come for me,' the girl wailed, struggling to free herself. 'But I'm not going with you.' Her struggles became frantic, 'Never, never, never.'

'I've come to watch over your father.'

'You've come to take me away.'

'I'm not taking you anywhere you don't want to go. Sit with me over here and tell me where you've been. Your father's out of his mind with worry.' She led a resisting Zarina past the cases crammed with tiny relics, then steered her behind the desk and made her sit in Alexander's chair. The child suddenly noticed the gun, lying on the desk beside a black Gucci bag. Fascinated eyes swept up and gazed into hers.

'That's your gun. I saw you scaring the man with it yesterday.'

'So, you've been watching me.' Samantha

slid the weapon into her bag and perched on the desk.

'I could see you through the attic window.' Zarina's arms were wrapped around the book. She was hugging it to her chest, like a shield.

'Which attic window?'

'The one in Nathan's cottage. I've been sleeping there.' Fear returned to her voice. 'You're not from the council or the police?'

'I've been sent here by one of your father's friends, to make sure no one harms him.'

'Alexander's not my father. My father's in Egypt.'

Samantha smiled down at the girl. 'You're a pedantic little thing. Your mother's husband, then; your stepfather.' She leaned forward, relieved Zarina of the heavy, leather-bound book and glanced at the spine. 'The Key of Solomon.' Amused green eyes gazed steadily into eyes that were brown and bright with fear. 'You should have taken the Grimoire of Honorius if you're really serious about summoning up the dark powers.'

'It's got a clasp and it's locked.'

'Just as well. It's full of occult and mysterious things. Dangerous even if you've been initiated.'

'Initiated?' Zarina's eyes were wide.

'Into the black arts.'

'Have you been initiated?' Curiosity and fascination were fast dispelling the girl's fear. She settled back in the chair.

'I was invited to be once, but I declined. It's wicked and dangerous; something one should steer clear of.' Samantha's smile faded. It was time to be serious. 'Where have you been? And where are your mother and brother and sister? Alexander's frantic with worry.'

'I've been hiding in the wood and the old stone quarry; eating and sleeping in Nathan's little cottage across the yard. I've been doing that ever since they were taken away.'

'Taken away? Who took them away?'

'Two women came in a car, and some police came in another car, and they all went into the house. I was playing outside. When I saw them, I ran into the trees and watched. Mummy told me to run away and hide if the police ever came, or they'd take me away and give me the chicken.'

'Give you the chicken?'

'She said they'd take my clothes off, truss me up to a pole and beat me and do bad things to me.'

Suddenly understanding, Samantha said, 'You mean as in Egypt, the Amned Duala, the Mukhabarat, the Security Police?'

Zarina nodded. 'Mummy said they hate Christians. Alexander knew the revolution was coming. He said things would get worse and we had to leave, so he brought us here.' Her mouth and chin began to tremble. She covered her eyes with grimy hands and began to weep. Her voice indistinct now, she moaned, 'But even here the police took Mummy away, and those women took Amir and Maria.'

Samantha lifted Zarina out of the chair, then sat in it herself and settled her on her knees. She wrapped her arms around her and held her close. The child had an earthy, animal smell. Burrs and fragments of bracken were tangled in her hair. 'Have you any idea where the women came from?'

'I think they must have come from the council. A while after they'd gone, two more women came in a van marked Beckminster Borough Council Social Services Department and went into the house. The first women must have sent them.'

'And you've no idea where your mother is?'

Zarina sniffed back tears. 'The last time I saw her she was fighting one of the women. The policeman and policewoman pulled her away and fastened her wrists and pushed her into their car.'

'Your mother was fighting one of the women who took your brother and sister away?'

Zarina nodded. 'I've never seen her so angry, not even that day she went to school about me. She was screaming at the woman, hitting her with her fists and pulling out great lumps of hair.' She groped in the pocket of her grimy blouse and pulled out a lock of brown hair that still had a patch of dried and scaly skin attached. 'I found this on the drive after they'd gone. There were others, but this was the biggest.'

'Is that why you wanted the grimoire?'

Zarina nodded.

Samantha felt an arm winding around her neck and a thin body snuggling closer. Their encounter, her questioning, seemed to be exhausting the child. And perhaps the days of loneliness and isolation had made her crave the warmth and affection of a woman. Samantha held her for a while, then whispered, 'Why don't we go up to your room and find some clean clothes, then you could take a nice hot bath and change?'

Zarina nodded again, then sat upright. 'How's Alexander?' She slid from Samantha's knee. 'I came across to the house after Mummy and Amir and Maria had been taken away to tell him what had happened, but some women in green overalls were pulling him about on the bed, trying to take his clothes off. He was moaning and crying and the room smelled of sick and poo, so I ran away.'

'He's much better now. Nurses and a doctor are taking care of him and the room doesn't smell any more, but he sleeps a lot.'

'Is he getting better?'

'He's not in so much pain now, but no, he's not getting better.'

'Is he going to die?'

Samantha met the girl's troubled gaze and was struck, once more, by the strong resemblance of the child to her mother. Beneath all the grime, she was quite beautiful. And she was obviously intelligent. A lie would be unkind. It would engender false hope, and in a few weeks she'd be saddened again. Taking her hand, Samantha said softly, 'I'm afraid so, Zarina.'

'Soon?'

She shrugged. 'The doctor thinks three weeks, possibly four, but these things are difficult to predict.'

'May I see him?'

'I think you should, but he'll be sleeping now. He usually wakes around three.' Samantha rose from the chair, picked up her bag, and they headed for the door. 'Let's see if we can find some clean clothes for you to wear, and some shoes. Then you can take that bath.'

'Would you stay with me?'

'Come into the bathroom?'

'Please. I don't want to be alone. Those women might creep up the stairs and take me if I'm alone.'

'I won't allow anyone to take you.'

Zarina slid her hand into Samantha's and they stepped out into the passageway that led to the stairs. 'And will you wash my hair? Mummy always used to do that for me.'

* * *

Samantha worked a comb through Zarina's hair, lifting it and allowing it to fall in the warm blast of a rather noisy dryer. Two changes of bath water, a manicure and clean underwear had made the child fragrant again. Her old clothes had been bagged, ready for Nathan to carry off to his trench, and she was sitting on a stool in Samantha's bedroom. The hot bath, the care and attention, seemed to have calmed her and lifted her mood.

Samantha switched off the dryer, laid it on the dressing table, then slid a dove-grey chiffon dress from its hanger. 'This looks very elegant.' She gathered up the skirt and lowered it over Zarina's head. The girl slid her arms into the long sleeves and drew it on.

'Alexander went with Mummy to buy it for

me; last year, before he became ill. I tried on dozens. He kept saying, 'Not good enough, not good enough.' Mummy was annoyed until he told her she must have a new dress and shoes too, then she didn't seem to mind so much. It was the expense, you see. It was frightfully expensive.'

Samantha began to fasten the cloth-covered buttons that ran down the back to the waist. 'And why did he buy you such a special dress?'

'I was to go with him and Mummy to a reception at Oxford University — Merton College. Mummy didn't think I ought to go with them, but Alexander insisted. He told everyone, all the professors and their wives, that I was his eldest daughter. I'm not, of course. He's not my father.'

'If Alexander isn't your father, who is?' Samantha handed her a pair of opaque grey tights. 'Take those white socks off and put these on. They go better with the dress.'

Zarina peeled off the white ankle socks, rolled up the tights and began to draw them on. 'An American: a tall, handsome, rich American. He's very important. He works at the embassy in Cairo.'

'You've met him?' Samantha fastened the white collar and cuffs of the dress.

'Sort of. One day I was walking with

Mummy down Qasr el-Aini when this big car stopped at the traffic lights. Mummy told me to look inside. There was a man in the back. He glanced up from his papers and stared at Mummy, then at me, but he didn't smile or wave. He just scowled at us. When the car had driven off, Mummy said, 'That was your father'. After that, I sometimes put on my best clothes and waited at the crossroads near the embassy on the off-chance I might see him. He drove past a few times. He saw me once, but he just frowned and looked away. He sometimes had a blonde woman with him who looked older than Mummy. Mummy told me she'd loved him once but now she hated him.'

'And Alexander's been good to you?'

Zarina slid her feet into grey suede shoes. 'Very. He talks to me and tells me things, fascinating things. He knows absolutely everything about everything. And he allows me to sit with him in his library and read his books while he's working, and he makes Mummy laugh when she's being mean to me so she'll stop. He's made her really happy.' She put one foot on the stool, then the other, while she fastened the straps of her shoes.

Samantha turned Zarina towards the dressing table, drew her hair away from her face and let it fall in dark gleaming curls down her back. Their eyes met in the clouded mirror.

'How do I look?' the girl asked.

Samantha rested her hands on Zarina's shoulders and smiled at her reflection. 'You look very pretty.'

'Shall I go in now?'

'Why not? If he's asleep or too drowsy to talk, just come out and go back later.'

Zarina turned and looked up at Samantha. 'I've nothing to give him.'

'Just seeing you again, knowing that you're not lost, will be the biggest gift you could possibly give him.'

5

Helen Wallace was gathering breakfast things on to a tray. 'Have you finished with your cup?'

Howard, her husband, glanced up from his book, a questioning expression on his face.

'Your cup,' she repeated. 'Have you finished with it?'

He picked it up, drained it, then reached over and put it on the tray.

'You've not eaten your toast.' She tipped the slices into a cereal bowl and slid the plate under it.

'I'm trying to cut down. I need to lose a few pounds. In fact, I need to lose quite a few pounds.'

Helen glanced at the book he was reading and saw names and dialogue.

'You're putting on another play?'

'In a few weeks. Cast are meeting this afternoon for a read through.'

'You said you'd fix the back fence. Another strong wind and it'll be completely down.' She stacked the sugar basin and sauce bottle on the tray.

'I've not forgotten. I'll get some posts from

Parkers on the way home and make a start after dinner.'

Helen let out an irritated little sigh. Another wretched play. The Theatre Workshop and the school were the only things he was interested in. She screwed the lid back on the marmalade jar. 'What is it this time?'

'*Wuthering Heights*, stage adaptation by . . . ' he glanced at the cover of the book, 'Adrian Summers. It's rather good. It should go down well.'

'*Wuthering Heights*!' She carried the tray over to a worktop and began to taunt him. 'And what part are you playing? Let me guess. The ineffectual husband, the cuckold, what was his name? Wait a moment . . . don't tell me . . . Edward: Edward Linton.'

'I'm playing Heathcliff.'

She dropped the tray with a crash, then turned and stared at him. Indifferent to her derision, he'd immersed himself in the script again. His dark hair was turning grey, she could see the start of a bald patch at the back of his head. His face was becoming jowly, his shoulders were sagging, his body had developed that middle-aged heaviness. 'Did I hear you say *Heathcliff*?'

He nodded absently.

'It's going to be a comedy, then?'

He gave her a long-suffering look. 'No,

Helen, it's not going to be a comedy. That's why I need to lose a few pounds. And I'll be wearing a wig and stage make-up. I think I can be convincing.'

'Who's the wayward wife?'

'Jane Spencer's playing Catherine and Veronica Upton's going to be Linton's sister, Isabella.'

'Wasn't Jane Spencer the milkmaid in that Restoration comedy you put on last year?'

He nodded.

'The one you ravished in the barn? You were both very convincing when you were rolling around on the straw. Your sixth-form pupils were so shocked they actually stopped giggling.'

'Seventeen-year-old girls do giggle, Helen.'

'And is there a lot of kissing and ravishing in this one?' She swung the dishwasher door down.

'A few love scenes,' he said patiently. 'Passionate with Catherine, more restrained with Isabella, but no ravishing. It's mostly cruelty and unpleasantness.'

Suddenly losing what little interest she had, she said, 'I'm thinking of visiting Alexander. I was hoping you'd come with me, but I suppose you'll be too busy rehearsing.'

'You're going to go down to Sourbeck?'

'Alexander's ill. Very ill. I ought to go.'

'Did Rasha phone?'

'The social services people at the council contacted me, a few weeks ago. I really ought to have gone before now.'

Howard laid the script on the table and began to pay attention. 'You didn't tell me.'

'You were busy with the end of term exams. You're very difficult to talk to when you're under pressure with exams.' She drained the coffee pot into the sink, stashed it in the dishwasher, then tipped his uneaten toast into the waste bin.

'But why social services? Why didn't Rasha phone?' He watched fabric tighten over firm and nicely rounded buttocks as his wife stooped down to raise the dishwasher door. Then she snatched up a spray bottle and cloth and began to clean worktops. The brisk movement made her breasts tremble beneath the ivory silk of her blouse. He sensed she was ignoring him, as she sometimes did. He was sure she'd heard him, but she seemed reluctant to turn and face him. For the first time that morning, he really looked at her. She'd put on her tight grey skirt and black high-heeled shoes and she'd waved her hair, done her face and clipped pearl studs to her ears. He suddenly remembered it was her flower-arranging and brass-polishing morning at St Hilda's. 'Why did social services phone?'

he repeated. 'Couldn't Rasha phone you?'

She put the spray bottle down. Without looking at him, she said, 'They came to see me.'

'Who came to see you?'

'The Beckminster Borough Council Social Services people. Two women.'

'They came all the way from Beckminster? It's almost two hundred miles.'

'They wanted to talk to a close family member, and I'm the only family Alexander has.' She turned, eyed him warily for a moment, then went on. 'They were concerned about the children, and about Rasha. They wanted some insights into the marriage.'

'Insights into the marriage?'

'Please don't repeat everything I say, Howard. It's so irritating. The headmistress at the children's school got in touch with the social services people and said she was concerned about the eldest girl's behaviour. She thought she might be disturbed. She said she'd reason to believe that someone was involving the child in occult things, and that she had a precocious interest in sexual matters. She thought she might be suffering some form of sexual abuse — from a man within the household.'

'Sexual abuse? Old Alex? That's utterly preposterous.'

'She's not Alexander's child.'

Howard gave his wife a look of outraged amazement. 'So what? Alexander wouldn't harm any child. He's a very decent human being.'

'There are many things you don't know, Howard.'

'What do you mean: '*Many things I don't know*'?'

'He's always been highly sexed. He was awakened too soon.'

Howard laughed. 'Awakened? What the devil does that mean?'

'It was when he was in his teens. I went into his bedroom and caught him with one of the maids.'

'Thirteen? Fourteen? Fifteen?'

'He was home after his first term at Cambridge, so I suppose he'd be eighteen, going on nineteen.'

'Then he was a man, not a boy.'

Helen bristled. 'He'd led a very sheltered life. In his mind he was still a boy. For heaven's sake, Howard, the woman had opened the top of her dress and unbuttoned his trousers.'

'Lucky old Alexander.'

Helen glared at him. 'Sometimes you disgust me, Howard. You're the father of a teenage girl and boy, and you spend your working day and most evenings teaching impressionable teenage girls. You, above all people, should know it's not appropriate for a mature woman to take advantage of a young boy in that way.'

'I'll bet Alexander wasn't complaining. So, what did you do when you discovered this debauchery?'

'Told Mummy, of course. I was only six or seven, so I didn't really understand what was going on, but I knew they were doing something terribly wicked. Mummy told Daddy, the maid was dismissed and Alexander got a good telling off. It didn't stop him. He used to meet the woman in the village. He went on seeing her, on and off, until she got married. And when I was older, when I understood these things, I could see he'd become obsessed with sex. I'm sure that's why, when he got tired of philandering, he married that awful Egyptian woman. They're two of a kind, one as bad as the other. No decent respectable woman would do the kind of things he'd want her to do. Really, Howard, how could he marry that dreadful woman and bring her and her illegitimate little brat into the family?'

'She's not a dreadful woman. She's very pleasant and kind, and she dotes on Alexander.'

'She was little better than a common prostitute before she married him.'

'She was a dancer.'

Helen snorted. 'Dancer? Shaking her breasts and pudenda in the sweating faces of leering, lecherous men? I don't call that dancing.'

'It was part of her culture. And there were women in the audience as well as men, and the men didn't leer. And I'll tell you again, your brother would be the last person to harm a child.'

'You know, Howard, you really are quite like him.' She laughed bitterly. 'Men! You're all pretty much the same. All you think about is sex. It's the only thing on your mind when you look at a woman. I'm not surprised you can be so convincing when you ravish your heroines on the stage. You don't have to act, it comes naturally; slobbering over Jane Spencer and shoving your hand up her dress like that. God knows what her husband thought about it all.'

'I didn't slobber, and I didn't put my hand up her dress. And her husband didn't think anything, because he knows it's just make-believe: we were acting.' He paused, took a deep breath, then, in a calmer voice, asked, 'And what did you tell the social services people?'

'That Rasha was a woman he picked up in Egypt, a woman who used to dance in sleazy clubs and behave like a common prostitute; a woman who, in my opinion, isn't fit to be a mother.'

'I simply can't believe you told them that.' Howard's voice had become ominously quiet. His wife's revelation had shocked him. After staring at her for a long moment, he asked, 'I presume it was the same social services people who told you he was ill?'

'They didn't tell me when they first came to see me. One of the women phoned me, about a week later; I suppose she was keeping me informed as his next of kin. She said when they visited Sourbeck Hall to investigate the complaints, Rasha became violent and the police arrested her. They kept her in the cells until she could be sectioned.'

'Sectioned?'

'Under the Mental Health Act. They've taken her to a secure hospital somewhere. The woman told me they'd found Alexander in the house, but he'd been so ill he couldn't understand a word they were saying. They arranged for a doctor to call and sent some council carers in. The woman phoned me again, a few days later, to tell me Alexander had cancer, probably terminal.'

'What happened to the children?'

'The social workers took them into care.'
'And this was weeks ago?'
'Two, perhaps three.'
'And you've not been to see him?'
'The council's put carers in. He's being looked after.'
'But what about Rasha? What about his children?'
'What about Rasha? And only two of the children are his. The eldest was fathered by another man. The wretched woman was no more than a common — '
'She's intelligent and charming and they adore one another.'
'Nonsense. He might adore her, but all she wants, all she ever wanted, is the house and what's left of his money. But she's not going to get it; not if I can help it.'
'I can't believe this,' Howard gasped, appalled. 'When your father died, Alexander asked you which share you wanted: the money or the house and contents. You said you'd take the money. We bought this house with it, dammit, and did it up and bought furniture and all the cars we've had.'
'And it's gone, Howard, all gone. Sourbeck Hall and the things Father and Alex collected must be worth a fortune. If we could get that and sell it we'd be comfortable for the rest of our lives. And we could give Timothy and

Hariett a good start.'

'But it's not yours. If Alexander dies it belongs to Rasha and their children.'

'You don't have to shout, Howard. And don't think I've not realized how much she captivates you. I've watched you looking at her. You really envied Alexander his slutty little wife, didn't you? But I'm not going to let some blousy, gold-digging tart and another man's child get Daddy's house and the things he spent a lifetime collecting. I'm going to make sure they stay in the family.'

'Whether you like it or not, Rasha, Maria, Amir and Zarina *are* family. You can't stop them getting it. And Alex isn't dead yet.'

'The children have been taken into care. Rasha's in a mental home. Apart from them, I'm his one and only next of kin. If I'm careful, there's every chance it will all come to me.'

'Jesus wept! I can't believe what I'm hearing.'

'You're pathetic, Howard,' she sneered. Then, fixing him with a withering stare, 'You could have made something of yourself if you hadn't wasted your life teaching at that wretched girls' school. We could have had our own money.'

'I've been contented there. I'm liked and respected by the staff and pupils, the girls are civilized and most of them are keen to learn.'

'And your salary's pathetic and your pension's going to be even more pathetic, and we've got to put Timothy and Hariett through university, and I want to set them up in life. We need that money, Howard. I'm going down to Sourbeck. Are you coming, or aren't you?'

He rose from the table, snatched up his script and turned towards the door that led to the hall. 'After what you've told me, I'd be too ashamed to look Alexander in the face. I don't want to be involved, Helen. In fact, I'd rather you'd not told me what you've already told me.'

'Don't you dare take the moral high ground,' she snapped. 'If it hadn't been for Daddy's money we'd still be living in that nasty little house on that ghastly estate and we wouldn't have two pennies to rub together. And I'm not letting some money-grabbing Egyptian tart take what belongs — '

When she heard the front door crash shut she tugged off her washing-up gloves and tossed them in the sink. God, what had possessed her to marry someone so easy going, so lacking in ambition? It must have been her hormones. She'd been young; nature had tricked her, made the first man who'd paid her any real attention seem so acceptable. That and all the love poetry he used to recite — he did have a first in English — and the romantic way he'd courted her. Such puerile nonsense. It all seemed so cringe-makingly embarrassing now. Mummy had liked him, but Daddy hadn't been impressed. He'd seen through him. He'd as much as told her he was just a dreamy academic, too pedestrian to ever do anything worthwhile.

She'd made one mistake, but she wasn't going to make another. She wasn't going to let some Egyptian whore and her little bastard get the family home and the collection and whatever was left of the money. While she was down there, she'd visit the secure hospital where Rasha was being kept, talk to the consultant, put feelers out, see what could be arranged. She'd lied to Howard. There was still some of Daddy's legacy left. She wouldn't be averse to speculating with it; using some of it, most of it, even, to ensure that Sourbeck Hall came to them.

* * *

The sun was asserting its mastery over another day. Paving stones were already warm, and grass and trees shimmered in the hazy heat.

Dressed in new jeans, a yellow blouse and white trainers, Zarina was taking Samantha on a tour of the mausoleum and the quarry. They'd just rounded the swathe of woodland that fronted the house and turned down a broad pavement that led, arrow-straight, to a white stone building about a hundred yards away. Broad ribbons of grass bordered the pathway. Tall cypresses created a sense of enclosure, intensified the silence and stillness, turned it into a secret place. The grass needed mowing, weeds had invaded the joints between the paving stones, but the neglect enhanced rather than detracted from the funereal grandeur of it all.

'I love your dress, the different shades of blue. You were wearing it when you arrived.'

'You were watching?'

'I was hiding amongst the trees. When I first saw you I thought you'd come to take me away.'

The sun was pleasantly warm on Samantha's naked back and shoulders as they followed their shadows towards the building. At its centre, massive bronze doors were flanked by lotus pillars surmounted by a solar disk on outstretched wings. A simple cove-like cornice crowned its windowless walls. Bit stark, Samantha reflected, but a rather clever evocation of things Ancient Egyptian. If the causeway had crossed sand rather than grass, if date palms had lined the approaches, they could have been strolling towards some mortuary temple in Thebes or Karnak.

She felt Zarina's hand reach for hers as they passed between shoulder-high sphinxes on their way up the steps. She gave it a reassuring squeeze and asked, 'Did you remember to bring the keys?'

The girl nodded. 'Alexander keeps them in the bottom right-hand drawer of his desk. The keys to the big storeroom are in the bottom left-hand drawer, in a cigar box at the back.'

'He told you where they were?'

'When he first became ill. He took Mummy and me into the library and showed us where they were kept.' Zarina held Samantha back when they reached the top of the steps, gazed up at her, and said, 'He became terribly upset when I went in to see him yesterday. I called him Daddy and he started to cry. He asked me where my mummy and my brother and sister were. I tried to tell him what had happened, but he was sort of woozy and I couldn't make him understand. He just cried and hugged me. In the end the nurse made me leave because she had to wash him and give him an injection.'

The child's dark and troubled eyes went on gazing up at Samantha for what seemed like an age, then she asked, 'Will you find my mummy for me and bring her back?' She was close to tears.

Samantha squeezed her hand. 'Your mummy *and* your brother and sister: I hope to fetch them all home.'

Zarina slid the huge key into the lock, but couldn't make it turn.

'Let me try.' Samantha grasped it with both hands and forced it round.

'I don't like it in there,' Zarina whispered. 'It's creepy.'

'You've been inside?'

She nodded. 'I asked Alexander to show me.'

Standing on tip-toe, Samantha reached up, drew down the bolt on the other door, then pushed on a pair of bronze handles. As the doors swung open, a beam of sunlight sliced through the darkness and swept across a carved and coloured mural that covered the back wall. They stood, hand in hand, gazing at the bas-relief of a stylized boat, its sail unfurled, its cargo a mummified corpse on its final journey to the land of the dead. A jackal-headed god was at the stern. A bizarre creature, part lion, part crocodile, was crouching in the prow. The figures were life-size, the sweeping lines of the relief carving precise and sharp, the terracotta-red and cobalt-blue as bright and fresh as if they'd been applied yesterday.

'That's Anubis, Guardian of the Dead, in the stern. What's the creature at the other end called?' Samantha's voice echoed around the high chamber.

'Ammut the Devourer,' Zarina whispered, awed and not a little frightened by the eerie strangeness of the place. 'Alexander explained it all to me. She's a goddess who gobbles up the hearts of wicked people so they can't go on to the Fields of Hetep — that was their name for heaven.' She pointed towards the shadows on their left. 'The woman sitting on a throne over there is the goddess Isis, nursing the infant Horus.'

Samantha looked across at the gilded statue. Sunlight gleamed on its horned headdress and pointed breasts.

At the other end of the chamber another life-size statue, well proportioned, realistic, made tall by the ears on its black jackal head, seemed to be striding out of the gloom. Zarina shivered. 'That's creepy old Anubis, coming to grab us and take us away on his boat.'

Samantha laughed. 'And what did your mother make of all this?'

'She hated it. Alexander brought her here

once, but she refused to go inside. She told him to lock the doors and take her away. She said it was a heathen place, haunted by evil spirits. And she wouldn't go into his storeroom. There are cabinets full of necklaces and earrings in there; and statues, and dried up bits of bodies in jars, and painted coffins — one's got a bandaged body inside. The air-conditioning has to be kept on all the time, night and day.'

'She didn't mind him showing these things to you?'

'I don't think so. She's always going on about doing well at school and going to university and becoming clever and wise like Alexander.'

'And how did you feel about that?'

Zarina wrinkled her nose. 'I'd rather be a dancer, like Mummy, but she'd never talk to me about it, and she refused to teach me. She's got a big cassette player and a lot of tapes. Sometimes she'd play them and dance for Alexander in the big salon. They'd light a fire and she'd turn the lights out. I used to creep downstairs and watch through the gap between the doors. When the music stopped she'd laugh and throw herself on him and start kissing him.' Zarina pulled on Samantha's arm, made her lower her head, and in a shocked little voice whispered, 'Sometimes she didn't wear anything on top; she was all bare.'

Samantha laughed softly. 'Perhaps you shouldn't have been peeping through the crack in the door.'

Zarina pointed towards rectangles of black marble. 'Alexander's parents and grandparents are buried under those slabs, and there are lots more empty chambers. His grandfather had the mausoleum built. The stone was the last to come out of the quarry before it flooded. A stream used to run through the woods — Sourbeck. It suddenly ran dry and the next day water began to pour out of a fissure in the quarry and fill the lower levels.' She tugged Samantha's arm again. 'Let's go. I don't like it in here.'

They stepped out of the gloom and coolness into bright sunlight and humid summer heat. Samantha made the doors secure, then Zarina reached for her hand and led her down the steps. 'I'll take you to the quarry now. If we cut across the grass and through that gap in the trees we'll come to the old road they used when they were bringing stone to build the house and the mausoleum.'

As they moved along what was now little more than an overgrown track, Samantha decided it was time to probe the child about more serious things. Making her voice casual, almost offhand, she asked, 'Did anything unusual happen before the social services people and the police came?'

Zarina glanced up at her. 'Unusual?'

'Something they might have heard; something that might have made them interested in the family?'

Zarina shrugged. 'There was some trouble at school about two weeks before the summer holidays started. That's the only thing I can think of.'

Moving in single file, they negotiated a stretch where the encroaching willowherb was waist high. When they were side by side again, Zarina went on, 'It was lunch break and I was in the playground. Three boys came up to me: Terry Bryant — he's a policeman's son — and Jimmy Mason and Bobby Carver. They were whispering to one another and laughing, and Terry Bryant asked me to let them do something rude. I told them to go away, so Terry grabbed my arm and said, 'Do it or we'll pull your knickers down.' I was sitting on one of those walls with a gap down the middle where they plant flowers, only most of the flowers had gone, and there was this big piece of brick lying amongst the soil, so I picked it up and hit him on the head with it. He yelled and swore and kicked me, so I hit him again, as hard as I could this time. He started screaming, saying I'd blinded him. Blood was running down his face.

'One of the women who watches us in the playground came running over. She told Bobby Carver to fetch a teacher and they called the ambulance and Terry went to hospital and I had to go to Mrs Hibbard's room.'

'Mrs Hibbard?'

'The headmistress. I told her what had happened. She made me tell her the rude thing, then she — '

'Would you tell me the rude thing?' Samantha asked gently.

'Is it important?' Zarina looked at her, embarrassed.

'It could be.'

'They told me to go with them behind the new classroom block and take my knickers off so they could have a look and a feel.'

'Really.' Samantha's kept her voice expressionless. 'Go on with the story.'

'Then Mrs Hibbard had Jimmy and Bobby brought to her room, but they said they didn't know what I was talking about; they were just playing tag near the wall and they hadn't even spoken to me. Mrs Hibbard sent them back to the classroom, then told me it was very wicked of me to hit Terry Bryant and then try to wriggle out of it by accusing him of dreadful things. She said I was in very serious trouble, and if Terry lost his sight I'd be in even bigger trouble, and she couldn't imagine what his parents were going to say.

'I kept telling her that what I'd told her was true, that it was they who were lying, but she kept on saying that no one else had heard them or seen anything and it was three to one, their word against mine.

'Then she told me to sit down on the chair that's in front of her desk, and she tap-tapped on the blotter with a pencil while she stared at me for a long time without saying anything. Then she asked me if anyone had ever behaved in an improper way towards me. I asked her what behaving in an improper way meant, and she said, 'Touched you inappropriately, or made you remove your clothing,' so I told her about Uncle Asheya.'

They rounded a bend in the overgrown track. Trees and bushes no longer blocked the view and they could see the rim of the quarry and the upper reaches of a distant rock face. The track began to dip. Soon they were descending into a vast rocky amphitheatre dotted with abandoned slabs of stone and derelict workshops.

'Uncle Asheya,' Samantha prompted. 'Would

you tell me about Uncle Asheya?'

'It was ages ago, when we lived in Egypt. We shared a house with my grandmother and her brother; I suppose Asheya is really my great-uncle. When I was alone with him in the kitchen, he used to slide his hand up my dress and say, 'Let me feel how plump you are. Let me see how grown up you have become. Soon I will teach you things; secret things. I will prepare you for life.' Then he'd laugh and show me his bad teeth and say, 'Not yet. Soon, but not yet.' He used to eat aish merahrah. It made his breath smell vile.'

'You mean the bread they flavour with fenugreek seeds?'

Zarina nodded. 'I think it must be the seeds. People who eat the bread smell like poo.'

'And what became of Uncle Asheya?'

'He kept pushing his hand higher. I got scared and sick of it and one day I told Mummy when she came to collect me from school. That night there was this terrible row. Mummy told me to sleep with her, and the next day we left my grandmother's house and went to live in a tiny room above a shop. And then Mummy married Alexander and everything changed. We moved into a beautiful apartment near the university, and Alexander arranged for me to go to a better school.'

Samantha studied Zarina's face. She seemed

calm and quite composed. Recounting events that must have been unpleasant and frightening didn't seem to have distressed her. She decided to continue the conversation. 'And how did Mrs Hibbard react when you told her this?'

'She said that it explained a lot but it was no excuse for the way I'd treated Terry. She told me to go and sit by myself in the room they use for special needs children while she made some telephone calls. Just before it was time to go home, she sent for me and told me that Terry Bryant wouldn't be coming back before the summer holidays, so she'd decided not to suspend me. She said she was going to have a meeting with my class teacher and when she'd spoken to Terry's parents she'd write to my mummy and arrange a meeting. She said she was taking a big chance not suspending me, and I'd got to watch my step. If she heard I'd been talking about grown-up things, I'd be out.'

While Zarina had been recounting events, they'd progressed along the track as it curved downwards. Now they were deep in the quarry. Before them was a pool, almost a lake, that filled the lower reaches. Sheltered by high cliffs, it was mirror-like and still. Another few paces and they were standing at the water's edge where the old track swept on down into the murky darkness. Samantha gazed across the water towards the distant quarry face. 'Is it very deep?'

'Alexander said it was as deep as two tall houses. He told me never to go near the edge because when you get away from the old track it just drops straight down.' Her face suddenly brightened and her voice became eager. 'Let me show you my altar.' She led her across the upper shelf of the quarry towards the biggest of the derelict buildings. 'It's over here, by the old sawing shed.'

They picked their way between abandoned slabs of stone, then climbed onto a flat table of rock about twenty feet square. Samantha stood at the centre of the circle and pentagram Zarina had outlined with blood-red paint, trying to make sense of the symbols daubed on the rock. They weren't astrological, and they weren't Hebrew. She smiled across at Zarina. 'What are these?'

'I copied them from pictures in the grimoire. That's why I needed it, and for the rituals and invocations, of course.' She pointed with her toe. 'These are the first five letters of the Enochian alphabet — that's the language of angels — and these are the names of the five infernal beings.'

Samantha held back a smile. 'And the purpose of it all?'

'To call up the spirits, to persuade them to destroy the people who took Mummy and Amir and Maria away.' Her voice had become driven; her slight body had tensed. She was holding her arms rigidly by her sides and her fists were clenched. 'I want to make them suffer, just like they've made us suffer.'

'And do you think the spirits will listen?'

'I know they will.' Zarina's face radiated conviction. 'I used the woman's hair and skin and blood in the ritual. It was such powerful magic, they couldn't ignore it. Once I called up a storm, and the pentagram I had then wasn't as good as this one; it was so badly drawn you could hardly tell what it was. I got the spell from one of Alexander's books, not a grimoire; I didn't know about grimoires then. The sky went black and there was thunder and lightning and I got soaked before I could get home. It flooded over the tank in the roof and water poured through the bedroom ceilings. I didn't tell Mummy I'd done it, she'd have gone crazy, but I told Alexander and said I was sorry about the flooding. He didn't get mad at me. He just laughed and said he knew who to come to if he ever needed a spell casting.'

'You said it flooded a tank?'

'There's a huge iron tank in the roof. They used to store rainwater in it. There's a big valve inside, like a metal football, that diverts the water when it's full. It had got stuck. When I got home, Nathan was trying to hammer it free. I'll take you up there and show it to you when we get back.'

'Tomorrow,' Samantha said, stepping down from the rocky platform. 'I have to make some phone calls, begin the search for your mother and brother and sister. And I must spend some time with Alexander.'

Zarina jumped down beside her and they began to climb out of the quarry.

When they'd reached the overgrown track, Samantha said, 'You didn't finish telling me about the incident at school. Did Mrs Hibbard send for your mother?'

'She sent a letter. Mummy didn't take much notice when she first read it. She was upset because she'd just got back from hospital with Alexander and they'd told her how poorly he was. She must have read it again later, after we'd all gone to bed, because she came up to my room, really angry, and asked me what it was all about. She came into school with me the next day. She'd put her hair up, wore the black dress Alexander had bought her for the reception at the university, and her diamond earrings and necklace and her very best shoes. I went with her into Mrs Hibbard's room. Terry Bryant was there with his parents, and Miss Cunningham, my class teacher.

'Mummy threw the letter down on Mrs Hibbard's desk and said, 'How dare you send me this libelous nonsense? How dare you accuse my daughter of lying?' Then she turned to Terry Bryant's father and said, 'It's your son who's the liar, Mr Bryant: a liar and a nasty little sexual predator.' Then his mother said, 'Terry wouldn't dream of doing such a thing. The thought wouldn't enter his head.' They all got really angry after that, and Mrs Hibbard had to bang on her desk until they stopped shouting.

'When it was quiet again, she said to Mummy, 'Zarina's clearly taken a distorted story home, Mrs Meyer. The truth is, she overreacted to an innocent playground taunt, injured Terry, then made up this story to excuse what she'd done'.'

Zarina pulled on Samantha's hand, led her off the track and through the gap in the row of cypress trees. They crossed the grass and started down the mausoleum causeway, heading towards the hall. Samantha could feel the warmth of the flagstones through the soles of her serviceable shoes. Insects were buzzing. The singing of a solitary bird seemed loud in the stillness. 'Go on,' she urged, her curiosity aroused. 'What happened then?'

'Well, by that time, Terry Bryant's mother had started crying and his father's face had gone bright red. You could tell he was really, really, angry. He told Mummy he was going to have everything properly investigated, and she'd regret calling his son names. Mummy just ignored him, turned to Mrs Hibbard, and said, 'Fetch the other boys in. Let's hear what they have to say.' Mrs Hibbard said that it was her office and she'd decide who was brought in, but eventually she told Miss Cunningham to go for them. Miss Cunningham was trembling and her face had gone all white. She seemed glad to get out of the room.

'While we were waiting, Mummy fumed and glared at Terry Bryant and his father. She didn't say a word, but she looked fabulous in the black dress and the diamonds, with her hair all gathered up. She'd put lipstick on and painted her nails, like you do, only she'd made her eyes much darker. She just stood there, with her hands on her hips, and stuck out her bosoms. She has big bosoms.' Zarina's voice lowered. 'They're bigger than yours.'

Samantha smiled. 'And when the boys came in, what happened then?'

'Mummy put on her coaxing voice, the voice she uses when she wants something from Alexander, and asked them if they were the boys who were with Terry in the playground. Mrs Hibbard told her that she was conducting the meeting, and that she'd ask the questions, so Mummy said it was her daughter who had nearly been violated, so she'd ask the questions. Then she put her nice voice on again and said to the boys, 'Well, were you?' and they said they were. Then Mummy said, 'This is a very serious business. You might both end up before a judge in a courtroom. You'd have to tell him the truth, so you'd be wise to start telling it now. And anyway, if you don't tell the truth, God will punish you. Now, tell us exactly what happened in the playground that day.'

'Jimmy Mason started crying, so Bobby had to tell them that Terry Bryant had said they should take me behind the new classroom block and hold my arms while he pulled my knickers down so they could all have a feel.' Then Mummy looked at Jimmy and said, 'Is that true?' Jimmy said it was, and Mummy said, 'What happened when you went over to Zarina?' He was crying so bad you could hardly hear him, but he told them when Terry grabbed my arm I picked up a brick and hit him in the face with it, twice.

'When he'd said that, Mummy looked at Terry's mother and said, 'Your little boy isn't the angel you thought he was, Mrs Bryant.' Then she turned to Mrs Hibbard and said, 'I think you owe me and my daughter an apology.'

'Mrs Hibbard's mouth had started twitching. You could tell she was really upset. Her voice was all shaky. She said, 'Nonsense. Zarina overreacted to a playground incident and almost blinded another pupil.'

''Overreacted? And what would you have done if three men had approached you and said they were going to remove your clothing and molest you?' Then Mrs Hibbard said, 'It isn't quite the same, Mrs Meyer.' So Mummy said, 'Indeed it's not, Mrs Hibbard. We're talking about an innocent little girl, not a mature woman.' Then she said, 'Come, Zarina. We'll find Amir and Maria and I'll take you all home. God knows what your father would say if he knew I'd put you in the care of this bunch of incompetents.' When we were going through the door, Terry Bryant's father yelled, 'What about my son's eye? He might still lose his sight.' And Mummy called back, 'Then he won't be able to stare at little girls' secret places, will he?' and we walked off.'

Samantha gazed down at Zarina, walking along beside her in her new jeans and trainers, her long and tightly curled dark hair gleaming. Her mother had won a Pyrrhic victory. She'd prevailed over teachers and a policeman, authority figures who'd never forget or forgive a public humiliation. And she'd paid a high price for it.

The house came into view beyond the trees. A minute later they were heading out across the wide forecourt. When the guard on the door saw them, he descended the steps and trotted over, talking into his two-way radio as he approached. Samantha heard him say, 'Miss Grey's here now. I'll put her on.' Handing her the radio, he said, 'It's Charlie on the gates. We've got visitors. He wants to warn you.'

Samantha took the radio-phone and held it to her ear. 'Charlie?'

'Two policemen are heading down the drive, ma'am: a Detective Chief Inspector Warrington and a Detective Inspector Bradden.'

'Did they say what they wanted?'

'Just that they wanted to speak to the person in charge.'

Zarina had overheard the message. She gave Samantha a terrified stare. 'They've come for me. Please don't let them — '

Samantha handed the radio-phone back to the guard, grabbed Zarina's hand and they took the steps at run. 'Go up to my bedroom. There's a pair of blue and gold sandals under the wardrobe and a blue clutch bag on the dressing table. Get them and drop them down to me in the hall. Then go down the back stairs and out through the kitchen. Find Nathan and ask him to close the doors to the stable where the big black car is being kept. Tell him if he can't lock them he's to nail them up as quickly as he can. When you've done that, go to his cottage and hide in the attic. Don't come down until I call you.'

6

Samantha waited in the shadows by the stairs, listening to the murmur of male voices becoming louder as the visitors climbed the entrance steps. After a sharp rapping, the door opened and the guard led two heavily built dark-suited men into the house. The younger of the two was black-haired with a pleasant, pink-cheeked Irish face. The older man's skin was sallow, his mouth down-turned, his expression one of tired irritability. Samantha emerged from the shadows, the heels of her blue and gold sandals tap-tapping on the checkered marble as she walked towards them.

'Two policemen to see you, ma'am.'

She smiled at the visitors then winced as the heavy door crashed shut behind the guard.

'Detective Chief Inspector Warrington,' the older man growled. He inclined his head towards his companion. 'And this is Detective Inspector Bradden.'

Her smile widened. 'May I see your identification?'

The corners of Warrington's mouth drooped

a little more. He wasn't used to being asked for ID. He groped inside the jacket of his tired-looking suit, produced a wallet and flicked it open. Bradden, whose suit was neatly pressed, his tie expensive, did the same.

Samantha studied the documents — images beside a printed badge of office, signatures beneath titles — then handed them back. Bradden's blue eyes and full-lipped mouth were smiling. The lines on Warrington's brow had deepened into a scowl. 'How can I help you, gentlemen?'

'And you are?' Warrington demanded, ignoring her question.

'Grey; Georgina Grey.'

'You're the owner of the house?'

'I'm not the owner. I'm here temporarily, on a care and protection basis.' She kept up the smile. 'Shall we go through to the sitting room? We'll be more comfortable in there.' She turned, presented a view of tanned arms and shoulders, a back that was naked above the flared skirt of her blue silk dress, and led them down a corridor. They passed through a pedimented doorway into the salon at the front of the house. Wine-red curtains, tied back with silk ropes, framed four tall windows. The matching sofas and armchairs were faded and marked here and there by the occasional stain, the Turkish carpet was threadbare in places, but the big sunlit room still retained a certain elegance. Samantha gestured towards one of the long sofas. ‘Please, sit down. And tell me how I can help you.’

Old springs protested as the men sank into sagging upholstery. Samantha drew a fragile-looking chair onto an oriental rug, settled it in front of the massive fireplace, then perched on it and crossed her legs. The furrows on the Chief Inspector’s brow deepened. Inspector Bradden’s bright-blue gaze lingered on her ankles and calves, then slowly rose to take in thighs curving beneath blue silk.

‘Care and protection?’ Warrington growled. ‘I presume you’re employed by the owners?’

‘By the government.’

‘You’re a civil servant?’

Samantha gave him her sweetest smile. ‘Sort of.’

Warrington sniffed dismissively. ‘What do you mean, ‘Sort of’?’ He eased his posterior off a broken spring. His world-weary, seen-it-all-before eyes were holding hers in an unblinking stare.

Exposure worried her. They were trying to place her, to discover her identity. She had to be careful. ‘Security services,’ she said. ‘The owner’s terminally ill and he was living alone. I’ve been assigned to watch over him and the house and its contents.'

Fleshy lips slowly shaped themselves into a smug little smile. Eyes still locked on hers, he said, 'Perhaps you could show me *your* ID, Miss Grey?'

'Of course.' She rose, went over to a small mahogany table, picked up her bag and groped inside for the wallet of cards. She slid out the only one she could let him see, clicked off the safety catch on the gun, then returned to her chair and settled the blue clutch bag on her lap. Leaning forward, she handed the card to the chief inspector. He studied the details. His partner stared down the front of her dress.

'Why does this place interest the security services?'

'Some of the contents could be bequeathed to national museums. There's a large collection of Egyptian antiquities here. Many of the items are priceless and the owner's extremely vulnerable. It's been decided that the house and the collection should be protected in a discreet way.'

'Who is the owner?' Warrington held out her card. Samantha leaned forward to retrieve it. Bradden took another lingering look at the shapes beneath the bodice of her dress.

'Professor Alexander Meyer. The collection was started by his father.' Samantha smiled. 'I hope you'll respect the confidentiality of all this. If word got out about the things that are stored here . . . '

'We won't mention it in our report.'

'Report?'

'On the murder investigation.'

'A murder!' Samantha injected a note of alarm into her voice. 'Near Sourbeck Hall?'

'Not that near: Howden Wood, a couple of miles away. We're visiting all the houses and farms in the vicinity, asking people if they've seen anyone or anything unusual. Thank God there aren't that many.'

'Someone was murdered in the woods?'

'Body was found by a bloke walking his dog. Dog started growling, pawed at a pile of leaves and uncovered it.'

'Man or woman?'

'Man.'

They gazed at one another across the sunlit silence. Bradden had managed to drag his eyes away from her and was looking around the room. There was a distant sound of a heavy door scraping across cobbles, a crash as it was heaved shut. Zarina had given her message to Nathan. He was concealing the black limousine.

'Naked,' Warrington added.

'Naked?'

'The body. Stark naked. Could have been

killed somewhere else and dumped; a car had been driven down an overgrown track that led into the wood.'

'Have you been able to identify the man?'

'Difficult. Face destroyed, upper and lower jaws missing — probably taken by foxes — so no chance of a dental check. Got his finger prints, but we can't find a match in the system.'

'Face destroyed?' Samantha gave the chief inspector a bleak look.

Warrington nodded. Samantha uncrossed then re-crossed her legs; allowed the hem of her skirt to rise above her knees. Bradden lost interest in the room and resumed his examination of her legs and thighs, gradually extending it to the sweep of her hips, her waist, the swell of breasts beneath folds of blue silk. 'So,' Warrington continued, 'we're asking if you or anyone else here noticed anything unusual, any strangers, over the space of the past four or five days?'

Samantha shook her head. There was the sound of hammering coming from the rear yard now. It was interrupted by the whine of an electric drill.

'You've been here long?'

'I arrived a week ago.'

'And you've been on the premises the whole time?'

'I've never left the house and grounds.'

'What about the chap who brought us to you?'

'Security guard; there are three of them. They watch the house round the clock, report to me more or less every hour. If they'd seen anything, I'd know about it.'

'Anyone else here?'

'The owner, Professor Alexander Meyer, the nurse who cares for him, a cook-cum-housekeeper who comes from the village, and a handyman who lives in a cottage at the back of the hall. We have our meals together and talk to one another; if they'd seen anything, they'd have said. The place is terribly isolated; no one calls, nothing happens. One day is just like the next. To be blunt, Inspector, we're all waiting for a sick old man to die, then we can wind things up and leave.'

Warrington nodded, then glanced at his companion. 'Anything you want to ask, Daniel?'

'The stuff that's been promised to museums; where's that kept?'

'In an air-conditioned store formed in rooms at the north end of the house. The windows have been bricked up. The only access is via an internal door. It's pretty secure.'

The chief inspector laid a hairy hand on

the arm of the sofa. Springs twanged as he heaved himself up. 'We'll press on, then. Just another two farms, and we're done.'

Bradden rose, dipped his fingers into his handkerchief pocket and plucked out a card. He smiled at Samantha. 'If you do happen to hear of anything out of the ordinary, perhaps you'd give me a call on that number.'

* * *

The blue-uniformed security man watched impassively as they swept past. The car slowed, they turned out on to the narrow lane, then accelerated away, heading for the main road.

Warrington sniffed. 'What did you make of that?'

'House pretty seedy and run down.' Bradden changed up through the gears. 'Incredible piece of arse, though. Very beddable. And she'd not got a stitch on under the dress, not on top, anyway.'

'I meant,' Warrington said tetchily, 'what did you make of the situation? Woman from the security services in charge of the place, guards, all that guff about protecting bequests to the nation?'

'You checked her ID, chief.'

'It seemed kosher. When we get back, put a

call through to that place they have on the Thames so we can say on the file that we checked her out.'

'We could go back tomorrow, get her to show us round the place, have a look at the stuff in the store, do a few interviews with the staff.'

'If she is who she says she is, we'd be wasting our time. And there's no way you're going to get your lecherous hands on her arse. She's a ball-breaker, Daniel, a right little ball-breaker. Jesus, did you ever see such eyes?'

'Wasn't really looking at her eyes, chief. I was too busy taking a butcher's at the rest.'

'Never seen eyes like that before: huge, green, boring into your brain, reading your mind. They didn't seem human; more like something out of a nightmare. Bitch could castrate you with a glance.'

Bradden laughed. 'You could always ask her to wear a blindfold.' Still chuckling, he braked gently. The car rolled to a stop at the junction with the main road. He waited for a tractor to rumble past, then pulled out. 'Let's have a fry-up in the canteen when we get back. I'm starving.'

'On second thoughts,' Warrington reflected, 'don't check the woman out. Let's keep quiet. It's pretty certain she is who she says she is.

She'll report back, and if the security services are involved in the killing they'll arrange for the body to be collected and we'll be asked to close the file. That'll tell us all we want to know and we'll have got rid of the job.'

'I don't think the security people are involved, chief. It's what you said in the beginning, a gangland thing. Body dumped in the woods after a payback kill.'

'It's the most likely,' Warrington agreed. 'But I keep thinking about the autopsy report.'

'You mean the way he was killed?'

'Yeah. Large bore powerful weapon, bullets that shred on entry and tear away the flesh. Pathologist said the first hit took the brains out, almost emptied the skull. The second shot destroyed what was left of the jaws and teeth, and there were powder burns on the side of the chest where the flesh had been blasted away. Why would the killer do that? Couldn't have been a bad shot, not when there were powder burns. Must have been removing some identifying mark, possibly a tattoo: funny place for a tattoo, though. And the corpse had been stripped naked.'

'I'm not following you, chief.'

Warrington snorted impatiently. 'Killer was obviously trying to conceal the victim's identity. The criminal fraternity don't usually work that way, they want the body identified to send out a warning. And where would they get ammunition like that? Stanley in ballistics said it's very restricted, even amongst the military. Idea is, if you hit someone, no matter where, the body's so badly damaged they can't keep on fighting.'

'Where is all this leading, chief?'

'I'm saying it's just the sort of thing that green-eyed bitch would have done.'

Bradden laughed. 'She's really got under your skin. Was it the hoity-toity way she asked for our ID, or was it because she's in charge and the security men were grovelling and calling her ma'am? You left Northcroft when they made Mary O'Donovan section head. You'd chew your own eyeballs before you'd call a woman ma'am. You were right the first time. It's a payback kill.'

'There's something strange about it all, something strange about her. I can feel it in my water.'

'Feel it in your water?' Bradden laughed helplessly. 'You're getting to be a right woman-hater in your old age, chief. That's your problem.'

'You can laugh,' Warrington growled huffily, 'but mark my words, any bloke who tangled with her could end up with his brains as well as his balls all over the bedroom floor.'

* * *

Samantha rocked to and fro in the swivel chair behind Alexander's desk, listening to the faint rustle of sound on the encrypted phone. The technicians must have sorted out the system; the clicks and bleeps had gone. She heard a rattle, the sound of breathing, then a male voice asked, 'That you, Sam?'

'It's me, Marcus. Thought I'd better give you a call. The police have just left. They've found the body in the woods and they're investigating.'

'Where's the body now?'

'In a morgue, presumably. I didn't ask questions; I let them talk to me. I'm pretty sure it was just a routine call, checking whether the locals had seen or heard anything. They asked for my ID. I didn't like that. I told them I've been sent here to watch over valuable bequests to museums because the owner's terminally ill.'

'That's partly true. Did they have a look around?'

'Didn't bother, and they didn't interview anyone else in the house, either. Like I said, I think they were just following procedures. A chief inspector, a man called Warrington, did all the talking. He seemed clever and shrewd in that faintly menacing way the police have.

The younger one just looked.'

'Looked?'

'Down the front of my dress and up my skirt.'

Marcus chuckled. 'If he'd been a gentleman he'd have been more discreet and you wouldn't have noticed. Do you want me to have a quiet word with the divisional commander; arrange to have the body collected?'

'They've no idea who the dead man is and staff at the Egyptian embassy aren't likely to report the men missing. I think we should leave things as they are. If you make contact they'll know we're involved. And they've got my ID.'

'It's false.'

'I still don't like it. I don't even like them having seen me.'

'Any developments with Alexander?'

'One of the children's turned up. I found her in the house. She's been hiding on the estate. She saw her mother being arrested by the police and social services people taking her brother and sister away, so she hid in the trees until they'd gone. She's the child Rasha had before she married Alexander.'

'Why on earth would they arrest his wife and take his children away?'

'I'm relying on the impressions of a child,

Marcus, but I think the authorities suspected abuse, came to investigate, and Rasha became violent.'

'Abuse?'

'It's rather involved, Marcus, and there's probably an element of retribution in it all. I intend to check it out. When I know more, I'll report back.'

'You're in there to get information out of Alexander while he's still compos mentis, not to get embroiled in his domestic affairs.' There was reproach in Marcus's voice. 'And we're wasting time. The illness is progressing. It could soon be too late.'

'I thought he was your friend, Marcus, someone who's helped you. Do you want me to put pressure on him; to threaten him? Would a dying man respond to threats?'

'Beguile him, Sam. Be with him whenever he's conscious, keep probing. Loretta's very agitated about the cost of all this. I had the devil of a job to get clearance for the research team you asked for. And the Americans are demanding daily reports. We've got to be able to give them something.'

'I've already told you, Marcus, the only way I'm going to have any success is by finding his wife and children.'

'If they've been taken into care, you'll hit a brick wall. Dammit, Sam, the children's courts and the social services people are more secretive than we are. And you can't lean on the authorities in the Department's name. We can't be seen to have any involvement in all this.' Samantha remained silent, listening to his exasperated breathing. Presently a resigned voice muttered, 'Okay. If you think it's the best way of getting the information out of Alexander, spend some time trying to find them. But do it on your own account, and keep a low profile. We can't be seen to be challenging lawyers and the courts and public officials.'

Having got what she wanted, she deftly changed the subject. 'You said you'd arrange for the car to be collected. It's parked round the back in a stable and I'd like it moved in case the police call again. They might search the place next time.'

'Later today or some time tomorrow. The driver will come in a car from the pool and leave it behind at the Hall. You or the nurses can use it until someone drives it back.' His voice became urgent, almost somber. 'There are other reasons why we can't waste any more time, Sam. We're pretty sure the Egyptians are planning to make another attempt on Alexander's life. And the South American cartels that supply the drugs can't be happy with the way things have been handled so far; they might decide to move someone in. We're talking about a major slice of the international drug trade. They won't take chances.'

'How long do I have?'

'Days. We're monitoring the situation. I'll keep you informed.'

'How many days?'

'Four, five, a week, maybe. After that I've got to give serious thought to the possibility of moving you.'

'Can you send more guards?'

'Out of the question.'

Samantha closed her eyes and tried to think. Every time she said yes to Marcus she ended up in an unspeakable mess. 'The man who's coming to collect the car: did you tell him to bring the ammo for a Heckler sub?'

'It's all arranged.'

'I think you'd better tell him to include two boxes of shells for my automatic. Ulrick the armourer knows what I use.'

* * *

Mrs Rasha Meyer screwed up her eyes. Strong sunlight, blazing through the iron bars that secured the high window, was burning her face, making it even more difficult for her to hold on to the fugitive thoughts that were drifting through her mind. Bright light was painful to her now. Like everything else, she found that difficult to understand, because she vaguely remembered having been perpetually bathed in sunlight that was far hotter and brighter than this.

She abandoned the struggle. Her thoughts were too elusive, swimming in and out of her mind like tiny silver fish, hardly rippling the surface of her consciousness. And her memories, impressions, sensations, were so vague and dream-like. Where was she? A helpless sigh escaped her lips. She had absolutely no idea. Who was she? She wasn't sure about that, either. There was a plastic band around her wrist with something printed on it, but no matter how much she tried she couldn't form the letters into words. She knew her name was Rasha, because the white-coated men and women who shepherded them about called her that.

Her gaze focused on other inmates sitting on blue plastic chairs on the far side of the room. Six pairs of eyes stared sightlessly back out of pasty, vacant faces. Three of them were placid, almost comatose; two were grinning; one seemed ineffably sad.

A movement attracted her attention. She shifted her gaze towards the corner of the room. The woman they called Maisie was standing there. Her lank grey hair had been crudely trimmed; the hem of her green cotton smock was low at the front and high at the back, and its unbuttoned top had slid over one of her shoulders. She was moving her hand to and fro while shuffling from one foot to the other; rhythmic, repetitive movements, rather like dancing. Dancing? The thought triggered a memory. Rasha tried to cling to it, but it just slithered away, like a tiny silver fish.

The old woman's face suddenly crumpled. She stopped shuffling, squeezed her legs together, then urine cascaded down from beneath her smock and splashed in a pool around her slippered feet. She began to weep. Men in white coats appeared, gripped her by the arms and muttered angry words as they dragged her away.

Soon Rasha would be taken to the place where they ate their meals, then to the rows of porcelain pans in tiny cubicles that had no doors. When that was done, they'd make her drink the bitter-sweet stuff from the tiny cup, then take her to the place where she slept.

She sighed. Sleeping and waking had become one continuous dream-time. Sometimes, after the lights went out, she thought she felt her gown being pulled open and hands squeezing her breasts. Then she'd shiver when bed coverings were drawn down and cool air touched her body and hands moved over her thighs. The real darkness would come after that: the uncomprehending darkness, the swift slide into nothingness. Everything was a dream. There was no reality any more. She relaxed back in her chair and allowed herself to float on the sunbeams that were blazing down into the hard, white room.

7

Samantha studied the face of the woman behind the desk. It was an attractive face, made more so by discreetly applied powder and a hint of lipstick. It was the face of a woman moving confidently into her forties. The earpiece of a telephone was tucked under a fall of brown hair that had probably been dyed to hide traces of grey. She was frowning, listening intently to what was being said, occasionally speaking in a low, earnest voice; guiding and giving directions. The jacket of her black suit had a faint pinstripe; her white blouse a V-neck. She was wearing a broad wedding ring and an engagement ring with a large and well-cut stone that flashed and glittered as she scribbled notes on a pad.

Beyond glass partition walls, staff in an outer office were sitting behind teak and chrome desks, staring into monitor screens or attending to paperwork. Half a dozen women and a solitary man were gathered in discussion around a conference table, their faces unsmiling, their expressions serious. This was a place of protocols, an organization constrained by rules and procedures, where grave matters were considered and the lives of the inept, the unfortunate, the vulnerable, taken in hand.

Samantha heard the telephone clatter down on its cradle and returned her gaze to the woman behind the desk. 'Mrs Carver?' The woman nodded.

Samantha settled her black and white bag on her lap and gave her a radiant smile. 'I understand you're responsible for child care in the borough?'

Mrs Carver returned her smile. 'Strictly speaking, that's Dr Suttcliffe, the director of social services, but I have day-to-day responsibility for the work of the child care unit. May I ask your name? The receptionist gave it to me but we were interrupted by the call and I — '

'Grey; Georgina Grey. I'm representing Alexander Meyer. He lives at Sourbeck Hall. More particularly, I'm trying to locate his wife and children.'

'You're in contact with him?'

'I'm currently living at the Hall, together with nurses and a housekeeper. He's extremely ill.'

The woman leaned forward, rested her arms on the desk, then arranged her face in a sympathetic expression. When she linked her fingers the big diamond flashed. 'I'm aware of the situation, Miss Grey, and I must say I'm most relieved to learn that someone competent is there. Are you a relative?'

'I've been engaged to watch over Professor Meyer and the house and its contents.'

'The family engaged you?'

'The professor. He asked an old friend to arrange nursing care and for someone to oversee his affairs. That's how I came to be appointed.'

The woman rested her chin on her hands and tilted her head back so she could take in more of Samantha's black and white sheath dress with its choker collar. She was trying hard to conceal her curiosity. 'I'm surprised he could. I visited the house with the senior caseworker a couple of weeks ago and he was quite incoherent.'

'He's lucid for much of the time now. The doctor visits him on an almost daily basis, and there's round-the-clock nursing. He seems to have improved.'

'I'm so glad you're there. We've been rather concerned about the situation. You know we had to take two of the children into care?'

Samantha nodded. 'That's one of the reasons why I'm here.'

Mrs Carver took a key from a shallow tray beneath the rim of the desk, rose and crossed over to a row of metal filing cabinets ranged along the only unglazed wall. She unlocked one, slid open a drawer and plucked out a folder, then leafed through the contents as she returned to the desk. 'Zarina, that's the name I was trying to remember. The eldest child. She's not in care and we're rather concerned about her. The caseworkers have been to the house at least three times and tried to talk to the father about the child, but he just mumbles, 'Gone back to Egypt.' I don't suppose you've any idea where she might be?'

Samantha shook her head. 'The professor's wife, the girl's mother, have you asked her?'

Mrs Carver frowned down at the folder. 'The mother, Mrs Meyer . . . ' she flicked over a paper ' . . . Rasha, has been completely uncooperative. In fact, that's putting it mildly. She was abusive and violent when the case workers tried to carry out an initial investigation. They've subsequently visited her in hospital and tried to question her about the child, but she's quite deranged.'

'Deranged?'

'She was sectioned under the Mental Health Act.'

'By the local authority?'

'The police arranged for her to be examined by doctors who signed the Section Two order. We liaised, of course.'

'Section Two?'

'Of the Mental Health Act. It was a compulsory admission.'

'And where is she being held?'

'That I can't tell you, Miss Grey. I only keep a few notes in here. The caseworker has the file with all the details.'

'Could you have it brought in?'

The woman gave Samantha a tight-lipped little smile. 'I'd have to take advice on whether or not that information could be given to you, Miss Grey.'

'Professor Meyer's dying. He's very distressed about the loss of his wife and children. Surely he has a right to know where they are and to be assured that they're being properly cared for.'

'I can give you an absolute assurance of that, Miss Grey. And the caseworkers have made two or three visits to his home but they've found it impossible to have a conversation with him.' The woman met Samantha's gaze for a moment. When she spoke again a faintly patronizing tone had crept into her voice. 'You see, you're not related to the family, and that makes it even more difficult for me to release information to you. We have to follow very specific guidelines put in place to safeguard the interests of the children. If you were a member of the family, even if you were a parent, we'd still have to be very careful how much we revealed.'

Samantha managed a persuasive smile. 'But when both parents are incapacitated by illness and when there are no other family members available to help, surely you could — '

'But the professor does have other family, Miss Grey, and we've been in contact.' She leafed through documents in the folder. 'Here we are: a sister.' She began to read a form. 'It would seem she's been most helpful to us, and we've kept her in the picture.'

'She'd know where the children and their mother have been taken?'

'She's probably been told where Mrs Meyer's being treated, but I'd be very surprised if she knows about the care arrangements we've made for the children. I'd have to confer with the senior caseworker to check that. Unfortunately, she's not available.'

Samantha raised an eyebrow.

'Mrs Meyer subjected her to a very violent assault when she visited the home. She was recovering well and was expected to return to work a couple of days ago, then suddenly she became quite ill again. Her partner phoned in yesterday to let us know she's back in hospital.'

'She was badly hurt?'

'The mother was frenzied, Miss Grey; completely out of control. She just leaped on Catherine and tore out great handfuls of hair. Blood poured from the wounds, ruined her clothes and the upholstery in her car. I gather her scalp was beginning to heal, and then, a couple of days ago, the wounds turned septic. They're keeping her under observation.'

Samantha recalled Zarina's fascination with the occult, her interest in Alexander's grimoires, the lock of hair, then dismissed the possibility from her mind. She was becoming fanciful; the social worker's relapse was pure coincidence. She met Mrs Carver's gaze for a moment, then asked, 'Is there anything, anything at all, you can tell me about the children?'

Mrs Carver pursed her lips, looked at Samantha thoughtfully for a moment, then said, 'Only that we applied to the court for an interim care order. The order was granted, of course, so, for the time being, the local authority assumes parental responsibility for the children.'

'And what happens next?'

The woman smiled. 'You're fishing, Miss Grey, trying to lead me on. The interim care order lasts for a maximum of eight weeks. If we're unable to finalize our report and proposals for the children within that time, we'll apply for an extension. An extension lasts four weeks.'

'And then?' Samantha asked.

The smile widened. 'We may have to apply for another extension.' She shuffled her papers and her tone became brisk. 'I really do think that's all I can tell you. As I said a moment ago, we're in contact with Mr Meyer's sister and we'll be keeping her informed of developments. I'll ask the caseworkers to urge her to get in touch with her brother and acquaint him with what's happening.'

Samantha rose and extended a hand. 'Thanks for talking to me, Mrs Carver. You're obviously busy and I have to get back to the Hall.'

'Perhaps you could contact me if Mr Meyer is having one of his lucid days? The caseworkers are hard pressed, but I might be able to arrange for someone to do an unscheduled home visit and explain things to him.'

* * *

A wave of heat rose around Samantha when she opened the door of the Ferrari. It carried with it an aroma of sun-baked leather and carpets; the fainter odours of hot metal, oil and petrol. The mid-morning sun, reflecting off the glass and chrome of parked cars, off the windows and bone-white walls of the enclosing offices, was dazzlingly bright. She took her sunglasses from her bag, slid them on, then stood beside the car for a moment, waiting for its interior to cool. Her gaze wandered up the building. Behind one of its many windows she glimpsed a face, framed by dark hair, gazing down at her. Mrs Carver was watching her leave. She lowered herself into the seat, swung her legs under the dash and slammed the door. As she'd expected, she'd learned little or nothing about Rasha Meyer and her children, but she had discovered that Alexander had a sister who might have been told where they were being kept.

Sunglasses shielding her eyes from the glare, air-conditioning cooling the car, Samantha found the inner ring road and headed west, out of Beckminster. Her irritation at the social worker's reticence began to fade. With any luck, Alexander would be well enough for her to sit on the edge of his bed and help him with his midday meal while she talked to him about his sister.

The last few miles of the journey back to the Hall were along a winding country road, deserted apart from a tractor towing a huge agricultural machine. She swept the Ferrari around a bend. Hedges became low and sparse. Across endless fields of ripening corn she could see the dark crescent of woodland that concealed Sourbeck Hall. A minute later she was cruising past the high stone wall that marked the boundary at the quarry end of the estate; past a bricked-up gateway and the boarded windows of what had once been a gatehouse and pay office for consignments of dressed stone.

Up ahead, on the opposite verge, a metallic-blue Peugeot hatchback was parked beneath the ivy-smothered branches of a dead tree. She applied the brakes, shifted down the gears and cruised past it at little more than walking pace. There didn't appear to be anyone inside. When she reached the junction with the narrow lane that led to the Hall, she reversed into it and drove back to the dead tree. The tractor she'd overtaken earlier was approaching. She waited until it had rumbled past, then climbed out and looked inside the blue car. It was empty apart from a newspaper and an AA book of road maps on the rear seat. The doors were locked. High heels rocking on the tussocky grass, she went round the back, reached down and felt the exhaust. It was quite warm. She slid her hand along the pipe. The silencer box was uncomfortably hot. The car hadn't been parked there for very long.

She could see for at least a mile in either direction along the road. It was deserted apart from the tractor and the ungainly machine it was towing. The low hedges allowed her an unobstructed view across more fields of ripening corn. No one was crossing them. She returned to the Ferrari, drove the short distance back to the bricked-up gateway and parked beside it.

Between the old gate pillars, the brickwork was at least eight feet high and capped with fragments of broken glass. The adjoining stone walls were a little higher. The curious and the unwary had to be kept out. Beyond the boundary, less than a hundred yards away, a wilderness of grass and bushes ended at the unfenced quarry edge.

Heavy timbers shuttered the two road-facing windows of the gatehouse. Picking her way through tall grass and nettles, Samantha approached the nearest and pushed at the weathered boards. They were rigid and secure. She walked on to the remaining window and pushed again. This time the boards gave a little. When she pushed harder, the shutter swung inside and a wooden wedge clattered down into the darkness.

The sill of the opening didn't quite reach her waist. After making sure the road was still deserted, she gathered the sheath-like skirt of her dress around her hips, clambered up, and swung her legs inside. She found herself on the business side of a sales counter. The remains of a roll-top desk, a table and a couple of spindly chairs were dark shapes in the gloom. Old box files and crumpled papers, covered in dust and debris, were scattered everywhere. On the customer side of the counter, encroaching vegetation obscured the view through a half-open outer door. A notice board, a cupboard and a third boarded-up window occupied the wall space on either side of it.

Samantha eased her dress down over her thighs, then swung the heavy shutter back into place. In the narrow band of light around its edge she could make out the massive iron bolts that had once been driven into sockets in the stonework. Someone must have scaled the walls then freed the shutter to provide a quick exit, or to make a future entry easier.

Her delicate shoes crunched on grit and broken glass as she rounded the end of the counter, pushed through the leaves and vines that curtained the outer door and emerged into the hot brightness of a small entrance yard. It was strewn with the rusting, briar-tangled remains of old machinery, overgrown with grass and nettles and weeds, some of which were shoulder-high. The wall across the old gateway closed off the end of the yard. On the far side, unprotected door and window openings exposed the long-deserted emptiness of derelict storerooms and stone masons' workshops.

She stood perfectly still, listening intently, taking slow deep breaths of the humid summer air. Only the buzz of insects disturbed the silence. There was no breeze to stir the grass or bring relief from the oppressive heat; there were no sounds of movement. All she could hear was the chirp of crickets, the occasional drone of a fly.

Perhaps she should summon the guards, instruct them to leave the Hall, one to approach through the woods, the other along the track that led around the mausoleum, skirting the quarry to meet her by the bricked-up gateway. Then she remembered her radio-phone was in her bedroom; she'd had no need of it while visiting the Carver woman in Beckminster. Anyway, it would take too long for the guards to reach her, and if an intruder was in the grounds the men would be better deployed staying close to Alexander.

Samantha gazed down the old cobbled

road that curved around the edge of the quarry. There were faint signs of disturbance to the grass and weeds and wild flowers that obscured it from view: snapped stems of ground elder, bent fronds of willowherb. Someone had passed this way not long ago. She clicked open her bag, wrapped her hand around the knurled grip of the gun and began to push her way through the encroaching vegetation.

After a hundred yards she moved into an area of head-high shrubs and bushes. When she emerged, she saw him, standing on the edge of the quarry, gazing down into the chasm. Medium height, broad shoulders, blond hair cut short, he was wearing a crumpled, cream linen suit. He suddenly stretched, reached behind him and scratched his back. The movement lifted his jacket, exposed the gun holster beneath his arm. She laid her bag in the grass, gripped the heavy automatic in both hands, then said softly, 'Stand completely still, or I'll kill you.'

His head jerked round. Startled eyes gave her a shocked, sideways look, and his body tensed when he saw the gun. 'No need for the pistol, honey.' He laughed nervously. 'There's sure as hell no need for a weapon like that.' He laughed again. 'It's big enough to — '

'Put your hands behind your head. Do it

slowly and keep them away from the holster, then turn and face me.'

He did as she asked. 'Can I just move away from the quarry edge, honey? It's one hell of a drop and — '

'Two paces. Slowly. Don't alarm me, or you're dead.'

He moved towards her. 'There's no need for this. I was just checking out the grounds, heading for the house, coming to see you.' He flashed her a reassuring smile, revealed his American obsession with white and perfect teeth.

'Coming to see me?' Arms outstretched, gun perfectly still, she held him in an unblinking stare.

'Tony; Tony Hueco, CIA. We're on the same side, just different teams. My people are getting edgy; they want to know how things are progressing.'

'What things?'

'With the professor. You need the information; we need the information. Didn't they tell you?'

'Tell me what?'

'Hell, what sort of an outfit do you work for? My people warned Marcus Soames, late yesterday, said I was coming, asked him to pass the message on.' He snickered out another laugh and began to lower his hands.

'There's no need for the gun, honey. Let me show you my ID. We can — '

'Put your hands back behind your head, then stay completely still.'

He took a pace forward. 'This is stupid. I'm from — '

'One more step and you'll be dead,' Samantha snapped. 'Do you think I give a shit where you're from? Get your hands behind your head.'

He linked his fingers behind his neck. Small blue eyes wary, his tone conciliatory, almost wheedling, he said, 'We're on the same side, honey. I know you. You're Samantha, Samantha Quest. Aka Georgina Grey. And I'm Tony Hueco. You must have heard of me: Chechnia, I was holed up there, watching the Russians.' His voice was taut and high-pitched; the words were tumbling out. Perhaps it was fear, or perhaps he was trying to distract her, playing for time, trying to stay alive. 'You caught a bunch of terrorists, interrogated them, left them for dead. We broke into the house after you'd gone; found the poor bastards, stark naked in the freezing cold, strapped to iron bed frames. One of them was still alive. We took him back to the village. When he came round he started screaming, 'I've seen the Devil. The Devil is a black-haired woman with green eyes and a blood-red mouth. Don't send me back to that sick Devil-whore.' He was out of his mind. Absolutely terrified.'

'Samantha Quest? Who's Samantha Quest? And who says I was in Chechnia? I've never been to Chechnia,' she lied. 'I've no idea who or what you're talking about.'

He laughed his high-pitched snickering laugh. 'You're dealing with an old hand, honey. I've seen the files, read the reports, followed your career. You're a legend.' He swallowed hard then drew in a breath. 'The Russian Minister for the Interior — Grasnev, Grosnoy, can't remember now — took the credit. They gave you a medal — no, not a medal, a fabulous fur coat. Shot every darned wolf in Siberia to make it; a gift from a grateful Russian people.' He laughed again. 'Hey, there's no need for the gun, honey. This is an honour for me, meeting the woman who — '

Powerful hands, big as shovels, reached out from behind her back, grabbed her wrists and jerked her arms above her head. Then she was lifted off the ground and shaken like a rag doll. She dropped the gun. Her captor dragged her arms behind her back, forced them upwards until the bones creaked then rammed a fist against her neck and forced her to her knees.

'You took your time. Another ten seconds and the bitch would have killed me.'

She felt legs like tree trunks squeezing her, holding her fast. 'Thought you were following me,' a deep voice growled. Another American accent: this one was Texas, not Washington. 'I heard voices. When I looked round, you weren't there. Crept back real slow, saw this black-haired broad sticking you up. Who is she?'

'Mercenary. Trained by the Israelis. Works for the British, on and off. She's called Quest; Sam Quest. Vicious little bitch. Absolutely ruthless.' He reached down, grabbed a handful of hair and jerked Samantha's head back. He grinned down at her. 'And she's a real babe.' He shook her head from side to side. 'Thought you'd be a prune-faced old hag, honey, thought you'd look older.'

The man holding her lowered himself until he was kneeling astride her. She heard a click. Sunlight flashed on a switchblade knife. A huge hand pressed it against her throat. 'Shall I?' the Texan growled. 'Then over the cliff and into the lake?'

Samantha's heart began to pound. The one called Tony was still holding her head back, still wearing his triumphant little smile. She fixed him in an icy stare.

'We'll take her to the cottage.'

'Too risky. Safer to get rid of her here.'

'She knows things. She might have started debriefing the professor. We need to question her. And the Egyptians are coming tonight: Jalan and Naguib. She probably killed Jalan's brother. He'll want to get even with her for that.' He snickered and jerked Samantha's head from side to side. 'We should keep her for a while; keep her until Renato Lujan and his boys join us.'

'I don't like it. We could be seen.' Samantha felt the blade pressing against her throat. 'Let's deal with her now, get rid of her. That way there's no come-backs.'

'Not now, Lloyd; later, after we've questioned her. And if we hand her over to the Egyptians, they'll owe us one, and maybe they'll be more cooperative.'

'I think I should kill her now. Someone might be passing when we take her to the car; she might make a commotion.'

'I'll back the car up to the open shutter. We can tie her wrists, gag her with something, push her down between the seats.'

'I still don't like it.'

'What's not to like about it?' Tony let go of Samantha's hair. Her head fell forward into the grass and the pain in her neck eased. 'Five minutes. I'll bring the car over. Just hold her there for five minutes.' He strode off.

The one called Lloyd settled some of his enormous weight on her, then removed the knife from her throat and flicked it shut. 'He did you no favours, honey. You won't look so sweet and smell so fragrant tomorrow.' She felt a huge hand fondling her breasts. 'Tonight you'll wish I'd used the knife. When the Lujans and their men arrive, you'll be begging to die.' He moved his hand down her body and began to tug at the hem of her skirt. It was too close-fitting to be roughly dragged up her legs. When a seam began to tear, he gave up, tightened his grip on her wrists and resumed the fondling and groping. 'Fragrant?' Laughter rumbled in his chest; a sound so deep it made the air tremble. 'Hell, no, honey. You sure won't feel so fragrant after — '

Samantha heard a thud, the cruel grip on her wrists relaxed and the man's great weight flattened her against the ground. She rolled onto her side, toppling him into the grass beside her. She saw his face for the first time then: fleshy, heavily jowled, the features big and masculine and deeply tanned. She turned her head. Above her, a dark and delicate face was silhouetted against the brightness of the sky. 'Zarina!' She lowered her gaze. The child was clutching a rusty iron bar in both hands. Samantha scrambled to her feet.

'I was going to my altar stone and I saw the man looking down into the quarry, so I ran back and hid. Then I saw you come out from the bushes, holding the gun. When the big man grabbed you, I picked up the iron bar and ran along the old road. The first man had gone when I got here, so I crept out of the bushes and hit this one as hard as I could. Have I killed him?'

Samantha stared down at the man. 'He's stunned, that's all. And he won't stay stunned for long.' She reached for the iron bar. 'How did you manage to lift this?'

'I had to use both hands. It's awfully heavy.'

'Go,' Samantha urged. 'Back to the house. Go into the library. I'll come and talk to you there.' She lifted the bar.

Zarina stared, wide-eyed and curious, her gaze flicking from Samantha to the Texan giant, prostrate in the grass. The man groaned, then slowly moved his hand towards his head.

This wasn't going to be a sight fit for a child. 'Go,' Samantha insisted. 'Run to the house as fast as you can. And don't say a word to anyone about this.'

Dark hair, dark arms, yellow blouse, disappeared into the bushes. The Texan was trying to rise now. Samantha swung the bar down, heard a crunch, saw bone yield. He moaned. She lifted the bar and brought it down again, and again, beating the man's face and forehead to a bloody pulp. Then, breathless with the effort, she tossed the bar aside and searched for her gun.

Coarse grass, summer-dried, laced with briars, spiked with weeds, formed a dense, concealing mat of vegetation. The man called Tony Hueco would be back in seconds. The gun had to be found. She trod over the area where she'd been standing when the Texan grabbed her, moving in a widening circle. Thorns tugged at her stockings, scratched the leather on shoes that were too delicate for terrain like this. She felt something hard under her foot, reached down and groped in the long grass until her fingers found the butt of the gun. She took possession of it, immensely comforted by its weight and power, then retrieved her bag and ran through the bushes, back to the cluttered yard behind the bricked-up gates.

Gears grated, an engine revved, its sound growing louder as the Peugeot was reversed over the verge. Samantha pushed through the curtain of leaves that obscured the pay office door, then crouched down in the shadows on the customer side of the old counter. The car's engine spluttered and died, a door slammed, legs brushed through long grass, then a beam of sunlight stabbed into the derelict office as the shutter swung open. A shoe scraped the window sill, someone dropped down and began to crunch across the debris on the floor.

Her back to the wall, a shoulder hunched against the counter, Samantha wrapped both hands around the gun and raised it. Tony Hueco's face appeared, an oval of sweating flesh moving through the beam of light from the unshuttered window. She squeezed the trigger, saw his head jerk back before he collapsed in a heap in the doorway. She remained perfectly still, watching the splash of blood and brains trickle down the whitewashed wall. Ears still ringing from the roar of the exploding gun, she listened for sounds of movement beyond the open shutter. There was only silence.

The bodies had to be searched, the Peugeot driven back to the strip of verge beneath the dead tree to await collection by one of the guards. When she scrambled to her feet her legs were shaking. She tried to brush the dust and grime from her skirt, but gave up. The smart little Moschino dress, the Blahnik shoes Crispin had helped her choose when they were in Florence, were ruined.

She suddenly longed to be back in her own

home, enjoying a meal with Crispin, listening to his silly chatter about the clients at his hairdressing salon; no longer threatened by aggressive men, but comforted by gentleness and normality. Marcus was a devious bastard. He'd known all along that this job would mean more than sitting with a sick man until he died. She must be brain dead to keep on listening to his smarmy talk. She had to stop accepting his lousy contracts.

Better get on. She crossed over to the door, knelt beside Tony Hueco's corpse and began to remove his clothes.

8

The vacuum cleaner droned, its tone rising and falling as the diminutive Filipino girl pushed it forward then dragged it back, slowly working her way over the expanse of green carpet. Another blue-uniformed girl, dark-skinned, delicate as a bird, was polishing a brass handrail on the stairs, making it gleam in the sunlight pouring through a window above a landing.

Helen Wallace sat back in one of the visitors' chairs, wondering how to put her request to Dr Asadi. She'd thought about little else during the long drive down. Howard was so useless. He should have been here with her, supporting her, helping her with this. He was the educated one. Why did he always leave her to deal with the difficult things? And it was her money, her father's bequest, that had bought them the house, the cars they'd had over the years, the holidays they'd enjoyed, paid for Timothy and Harriett's school fees. They could never have done all those things on his salary.

He'd been such a fool, spending his best years teaching at that wretched girls' school.

But the place consumed him; that and his amateur theatricals. So much education, a first from Oxford, and what had it got him? Just the monotonous routine of teaching the same old syllabus to silly teenage girls, for very little financial reward. And her brother hadn't done much better: a life wasted in tombs and excavations, museums and academia, with nothing to show for it except a few antiquities and a libidinous marriage to a vulgar Egyptian tart.

The rattle of crockery on a trolley, the thud of doors swinging shut, echoed down from the upper floor. A cup of tea would be nice. She studied the collection of photographs beside her on the wall: the dark, refined features of Dr Karif Asadi, a smiling senior nurse, an unsmiling head of administration, a group shot of the entire staff, taken in the hall at the foot of those sweeping stairs. Her gaze shifted to the magazines, neatly arranged on a low table: *Mental Health Quarterly, The Journal of Mental Health, Southern Counties Magazine*. She wondered if they were ever read.

What should she say to Dr Asadi? More precisely, how should she say it? It was such a delicate matter. She ran her hand down the pleats of her rather short skirt and picked a speck of lint from the sleeve of her bolero jacket. It was her very best suit: dark-blue, designer label, Harvey Nichols in Leeds; half price in the sales. It had still been unbelievably expensive. She hadn't wanted to travel down in it, but one had to look decent when meeting professional people.

Howard had been surprised when he'd seen her coming down the stairs with her case, wearing her best suit and the white blouse with navy-blue piping around the edges of the frills. He'd presumed she was going straight to Sourbeck Hall. She hadn't told him she was going to stop off on the way down and see Dr Asadi. She certainly hadn't mentioned their little arrangement. Telling him about the conversations she'd had with the social workers had angered him enough. God, he was so naive, so honourable, always so determined to do the decent thing. What about her? What about his children? There were times when family came first. That was why she was here. She was trying to make sure the things her father had handed down stayed in the family. But Howard couldn't see it. He simply couldn't.

A door with an obscure-glazed upper panel opened and a white-haired woman in a green print dress emerged. Her cheeks were pink. There were damp patches under her arms and beads of perspiration gleamed above her upper lip. 'Dr Asadi is back from the wards now, Mrs Wallace. I'll take you through.'

Helen rose, gathered up her bag and followed the plump woman across the hallway. They entered a tiny vestibule, then passed through a second door into a spacious consulting room.

Dr Asadi glanced up from a folder lying open on his desk, smiled and gestured towards a chair. 'Mrs Wallace! Please, sit down. I'm sorry you've been kept waiting; I was on my rounds. You wish to see Mrs Meyer, your sister-in-law? She's being given a meal at the moment, but I'm sure we can — '

Helen shook her head. 'Later, perhaps. I really came to talk to you.'

He relaxed back in his chair, pressed his fingertips together and gave her an encouraging smile. His teeth seemed incredibly white; his mouth was framed by a narrow moustache that curved down to a short, neatly trimmed beard.

Helen squeezed her legs together. She needed the ladies' room. Such a long drive down. Dark and gentle eyes were gazing at her expectantly. Deciding to proceed slowly towards the thing that concerned her, she said, 'The order committing my sister-in-law will expire shortly. I take it there won't be any problems extending her stay?'

Dr Asadi shook his head. 'None at all. It will be as we agreed.' He held her gaze. Although her lips were full and well shaped, her mouth seemed a little prim; the blue eyes searching his face apprehensive. No longer young, he mused, but very attractive in that reserved, middle-class kind of way. Her gently waved auburn hair, her tiny hands, her surprisingly frivolous blouse — the whole effect was quite captivating. And that aura of prim respectability intrigued and somehow challenged him. She seemed unsure of herself. It was as if something were troubling her but she didn't quite know how to put it into words. She crossed her legs. They were slender legs, with small feet and well-turned ankles. He guessed the thighs beneath her rather short skirt would be full and shapely rather than scrawny.

Becoming uncomfortable in the silence, he tried to restart the conversation. 'I think I explained the procedure when we made our arrangement. Mrs Meyer was committed under Section Two of the Mental Health Act: I shall extend her stay under Section Three. That would enable me to hold her here until the New Year. Keeping her here longer than that would be difficult.'

'In what way would it be difficult, Doctor?'

'I would have to show a clear, clinical need.

So far as I can see, there is none. Her behaviour hasn't caused concern. She was profoundly distressed about her husband's illness and over-reacted when officials called about the children. When they said they were taking them into care, she became hysterical. A not unnatural reaction.' Dr Asadi smiled and pressed the tips of his long slender fingers together again. 'Another five or six months; I think I've honoured our agreement.'

Helen nodded. She couldn't argue. She gazed down at the black leather handbag on her lap. Persuading him to arrange those extra months had cost her a great deal of money. It had really eaten into what was left of her father's legacy. But she needed Alexander dead, his funeral over, the legalities well and truly settled, before Rasha appeared on the scene again. The social services people had said his death seemed imminent, but he was lingering on. January, February — it might not be long enough. And Rasha wasn't stupid. If she returned home, she'd resume control of things.

She glanced up, saw Dr Asadi looking at her in what she took to be a rather detached way. Tall, lean, broad-shouldered, white coat open to reveal a dark and well-cut suit; his stethoscope, his badge of office, clipped around his neck. The dark eyes were so sympathetic, the beard, the gentle face, so Arabic, so . . . exotic! She found him almost indecently handsome; certainly much too handsome for a doctor. She'd be embarrassed if she had to undress and be examined by him. Deciding to take the plunge, she said, 'It would be very helpful to me, Doctor, if Rasha could be committed permanently.'

His eyebrows rose.

'Inheritance,' she explained. 'My father's estate.'

'Ah.' He smiled his understanding.

'How much would you require to . . . ?' She let the words hang in the air.

Isolated by the lobby, the room was completely silent and very private. A floor-to-ceiling window looked out over a light well where small shrubs and plants flourished around a tiny circular pool. A half-folded screen partly concealed an examination couch. A trolley laden with trays of medical paraphernalia stood beside it.

Dr Asadi cleared his throat. 'It would be extremely difficult for me to arrange a further extension, Mrs Wallace. Other professionals are involved in the certification procedure. They could ask searching questions.' He frowned, paused for thought, then went on. 'Unless we began to make appropriate entries in her records; prepared the ground, so to speak; took steps to ensure we had sound clinical reasons for extending her stay. But that would have to be very carefully managed.'

'You're telling me it's not impossible?'

'Not impossible, just extremely difficult. And I'm sure you'll understand when I say it would involve me in considerable personal risk.'

Helen gave him a nervous smile. 'Could you quantify the risk?'

'Are you asking me how much it would cost?'

She nodded.

He pursed his lips, placed his fingertips beneath his chin and gazed up at the ceiling. After a few moments' thought, the brown eyes swept down and captured hers. He quoted a figure.

Helen was shocked. It was more than ten times what she'd already given him. What was left of her money wouldn't come close to covering it.

Dr Asadi studied the frills on her blouse, her short pleated skirt, her dark-stockinged legs. When he glanced up he saw the disappointment etched on her face. He gave her a sympathetic smile, and said, 'I gather this is very important to you?'

She nodded.

'And I sense it's not just the money, it's a matter of principle, of family honour?'

She nodded again, then looked down at her bag and sighed. 'But there's no way I could raise that amount of money.'

'Perhaps we could come to some mutually convenient arrangement?'

'You mean defer the payment until I get the inheritance?'

He smiled. How could she be so naive? 'That's not quite what I had in mind, Mrs Wallace. As I said, I would be exposing myself to great risk. I would have to secure the cooperation, and ensure the silence, of others. The law regulating wills and probate and inheritance is complicated. And even if Mrs Meyer were to be permanently confined here, it's by no means certain you would benefit from your brother's death.' He studied the papers in the folder. 'There are three children?'

'Only two are my brother's. The eldest is from an earlier liaison. They're all in care.' She brushed a lock of hair from her cheek and swept it behind her ear. 'The social services people have been in touch with me; kept me informed. They're extending the care orders until they can complete their report. I understand they're going to recommend adoption. They tell me they'll have no difficulty placing them; they're just waiting for Alex to die and the medical report on Rasha. I think we agreed your report would encourage them to proceed with adoption.'

'Indeed we did, Mrs Wallace, and that will be taken care of. Even so, it's by no means certain you'll inherit.'

Helen sighed out her disappointment and gathered up her bag. 'I'm wasting your time, Dr Asadi. There's no way I could find that amount of money, and I wouldn't dare borrow it.'

'When I suggested we come to an arrangement, I didn't have money in mind, Helen. May I call you Helen?'

She looked bemused. 'Of course, but I don't see — '

Amazed now by her failure to grasp what he was suggesting, but not wanting to outrage her delicacy, he chose his words with care. 'Business transactions between men and women don't have to be based exclusively on money, Helen.'

She stared at him, her expression uncomprehending.

He made his voice particularly gentle. 'You're a very attractive woman, Helen. Perhaps we . . . ' He smiled and shrugged.

Helen couldn't believe what she was

hearing. Was he really propositioning her? Her cheeks flamed.

Dr Asadi watched the crimson tide flow down her throat and disappear amongst the frills bursting from her smart little jacket. He'd shocked her; shocked her to the core, as they say. He found her embarrassment strangely arousing. This could be a fascinating experience, persuading her to trust him, to shed her inhibitions and relax with him. He continued to smile at her.

'I'm a married woman, Doctor. I have children, I — '

'Must your life be so ordinary? And do you have to live it like an open book? Surely you're allowed some secrets? You're miles away from home. No one knows you and you have every reason to come here while your brother is ill, while you sort out his estate; every reason to come down and stay for a few days, for a weekend, for a whole week, even.'

Helen let out an embarrassed little laugh. 'I simply can't believe what you're suggesting to me, Doctor.'

'You can't believe that I find you attractive?'

'Well . . . no, not in that way. I'm married, for heaven's sake. I have two teenage children. I have no experience of this sort of thing. I'm no longer young.'

'Does a woman have to be young to be attractive? I find you very attractive, Helen. Quite beautiful, in fact.'

'I think we should stop the conversation there, Dr Asadi.' Still blushing and extremely flustered, she rose to her feet.

'Think about it, Helen. Don't dismiss it out of hand.'

'This arrangement,' she demanded, curious despite herself, 'when would it start? More important, perhaps, when would it finish?'

'It would start as soon as you agreed to it, but in days rather than weeks; you couldn't expect me to wait too long. It would continue until you had your inheritance. After that it would be up to you.'

'That could be months; years even. I might never get the wretched inheritance.'

'Precisely, Helen. That's what I was trying to tell you a moment ago. With this arrangement, I would at least receive some recompense for the risks I was taking. If the outcome was successful, you could pay me half the figure I suggested and be released from it.'

'That's completely outrageous.'

Dr Asadi stopped smiling. 'I would be risking a very great deal for you, Helen. My professional reputation, my career, my earnings for the rest of my life; it would all be laid on the line. I think I'm being generous. I'm trying my best to help you. And what makes you so sure you'd find such an arrangement distasteful? Do you find me utterly repulsive?'

'I'm a married woman, Doctor. I have teenage children. And it may surprise you to know that I have very little sexual experience.'

'And what makes you think I would wish you to be experienced?'

'I'd have absolutely no idea how to behave, how to conduct myself. I wouldn't know what to do.'

He began to laugh, softly and without derision. 'Mrs Wallace — Helen — every mature adult knows what to do. Your instincts, your feelings, your sensations, would inform you.' He'd pressed her enough. Her face and neck were suffused by a deep blush and embarrassment had brought her close to tears. It was time to change the subject. Rising to his feet, he rounded the desk and said, 'Perhaps you would like me to take you to see your sister-in-law?'

Helen shook her head. 'I'd rather not. I'm content to leave her in your care.' Face burning, she almost ran towards the door. He moved past her and opened it. As she was stepping into the tiny lobby, he said, 'Please think about my suggestion, Helen. Don't dismiss it out of hand. And if you change your mind, call me. My private number's written on the card I gave you.'

* * *

Samantha stood behind Alexander's desk, gazing into the walled orchard. The sun was blazing out of a cloudless sky, gleaming on ripening fruit, casting deep shadows beneath the trees, making the apples seem like drops of blood suspended above dark pools.

Closing her eyes against the brilliant light, it suddenly occurred to her that all the defining moments of her life had been marked by sunlight and brightness; it made the memories more vivid. Her father's sudden death in the gleaming whiteness of that hospital ward in Jerusalem. Being taken to Sister Anunciata's sunlit study to be told her mother had died the previous night. The blinding flash that tore apart the bus that was carrying her half-sister, her brother-in-law, her niece, across Berlin. Her summer wedding reception in the hotel on Mount Carmel, high above the Bay of Haifa, her new mother-in-law livid because a Gentile in a cheap satin suit, a goy, a stupid little shiksa, had stolen her handsome doctor son. Her eyes blinded by sunlight, screaming her husband's name as she ran across a field towards men bearing a stretcher, only to discover that he was already dead.

She'd once overheard one of her father's chess-playing friends say, 'Jacob Kwestrovitch, life's a shit sandwich. The thicker the bread, the easier it is to swallow.' She'd had all the bread she could possibly want: exotic cars, fine clothes, travel, luxurious hotels; but there were still things she found hard to swallow. She shivered. Things like her brush with death less than an hour ago.

A phone on the desk began to bleep; bleep, not ring. It was the encrypted mobile. She turned and snatched it up. 'Marcus?'

'You left a message. You asked me to call.'

'I discovered two intruders in the grounds this morning. American nationals. One was carrying a CIA card,' she reached over the desk and took a passport from a pile of documents. 'He was called Tony Hueco. The other man had an FBI badge in his wallet.' She tossed the passport down and took square of plastic from a second pile. 'He called himself Lloyd Harman.'

'Where are they now?'

'Dead. Stripped down to their underpants and hidden in long grass.'

'You killed them?'

'I had to. When I challenged them, they threatened to kill me. Do you want to have the bodies collected?'

'Best not talked about. Don't mention it in any reports. Can you deal with the disposal?'

'I'll do it tonight. I'll seal their papers and personal things in separate envelopes and send them to you. They were carrying a hundred and ten thousand pounds in an attaché case. I'll send that with the documents, minus two thousand.'

'Minus two thousand?'

'I was wearing a Moschino dress and Blahnik shoes. They were almost new. Someone built like a gorilla pulled the stitching on the skirt, the shoes are scuffed and everything's grass-stained and covered in grime.'

'You can't appropriate funds like that, Sam. And it's not the first time. The monies should come to me intact. And two thousand pounds for a frock and a pair of shoes?'

'That doesn't cover what I paid. And you're never willing to authorize replacements. Damn it, Marcus, I was within two seconds of having my throat cut by the big hairy bastard.'

'I don't think Charlotte's ever paid more than a hundred pounds for a frock.'

'And she strides around the farm in wellington boots. I'm one of your agents, Marcus, not your wife. I'm keeping the cash for the dress and shoes.'

'Why the devil were you roaming the grounds in a Meccano dress and Blunket shoes?'

'Moschino and Blahnik. I'd been into Beckminster, on business. When I arrived back I saw a car parked near some bricked-up gates at the rear of the estate and went in to investigate. And don't tell me what to wear, Marcus.'

He injected a note of concern into his voice, trying to placate her. 'Are you okay, Sam?'

'No, I'm not okay. The CIA man knew who I was. He said they've got a file on me, gave me a potted biography. Who was stupid enough to broadcast the fact that I'm here?'

A silence ended in a sigh. 'The Americans are becoming very agitated. They want a result as desperately as we do. They're putting pressure on us through the Foreign Office. Loretta had to give assurances to the Cabinet. She made it known that all possible measures had been taken to ensure Alexander's well-being, and that she'd assigned our best operative to oversee his protection and obtain information.'

'She mentioned me by name?'

'She might have done, but anyone who understands these things could have inferred it was you from what was said.'

'The Americans have a file on me, Marcus. They may have photographs.'

'The intelligence services of every major nation will have a file on you, Sam. Whether or not they have photographs, I can't say, but having regard to the way you've operated, I very much doubt it.'

Samantha didn't speak. She just closed her eyes and listened to the faint clicks and bleeps of the encryption while she reflected on what he'd said. She didn't like it. She didn't like it at all.

'They're dead, Sam,' he reminded her gently. 'They can't report on who or what they've seen to anyone. When I get the papers, I'll have them checked out. I've no knowledge of anyone being sent to the UK. They're probably not what they seem.'

'They mentioned a cottage, presumably not far from here. They said two Egyptians were arriving tonight, some other men later.'

'Different factions. They don't trust one another, so they all want to get involved. We heard things were stirring. Perhaps it's time we moved you all out. Problem is, finding somewhere to move you to. Has Alexander had anything to say?'

'He's awake and lucid for two or three hours most afternoons now, but he just keeps asking for his wife and children. That's all he wants to talk about. We won't learn anything until I've resolved those issues.'

'You've pressed him for information?'

'I've tried to steer the conversation. I've used every verbal trick, played every little mind game in the book. He's not saying anything.'

'If the situation deteriorates, you've got to close in and do whatever's necessary to make him talk.'

'Deteriorates?'

'If you sense he's coming close to death, or if things become dangerous, you've got to make it plain to the silly old bugger that it's his duty to pass on the information.'

'The situation's already dangerous. And this man's your friend. Surely you don't expect me to — '

'We're sometimes called on to do things for a greater good, Sam. I'm ordering you to get the information.'

Bastard! Samantha fumed, then said, 'No one's been to collect the embassy car.'

'One of the couriers is coming. They've been under pressure or we'd have had someone there sooner. Carstairs is organizing it. He'll pass on the stuff you requisitioned.'

'Has the courier left yet?'

'He won't leave until three. Should be with you around five.'

'Tell him to bring half a dozen body bags; the sort of thing the navy uses for burials at sea.'

'Might not manage that particular type. I'll send you what I can get hold of. And Sam . . . Sam?'

'I'm still here, Marcus.'

'For Christ's sake get the information out of Alexander. Loretta's fuming about the delay and the cost, and the Americans, the French and now the Spanish are becoming very agitated, to say the least.'

Samantha switched off the phone, tossed it down on the desk and sank into Alexander's chair. Her gun, stripped down to its component parts, was laid out on the blotter. She frowned down at it. The solvent should have softened the powder deposits by now. She drew on a pair of cotton gloves, began to work an old toothbrush over the frame, then dried it with a paper towel and applied oil from a tiny squeeze-bottle. She repeated the process with the slide, the recoil spring, the barrel and chamber. Then, with quick deft movements, began to put the parts back together. Such a wicked device, she reflected; so simple, yet so powerful. And so deadly.

She heard a faint sound and glanced up. A face had appeared above the back of the leather sofa and curious eyes were watching her reassemble the gun.

'How long have you been there, Zarina?'

'A while. Ever since I got back to the house. You told me to come here.'

'So I did.' Samantha smiled, wondering how much the child had overheard, how much of it she'd understood.

'I've been reading.'

'Not a grimoire?'

'*Anne of Green Gables.* It's about a girl with red hair. Alexander gave it to me. He's given me a lot of books. I like to lie here and read.'

'You overheard my conversation.'

'I can keep secrets.'

Samantha slid the ammunition clip into the butt and drew back the slide. The topmost round clicked into the chamber. 'The things you've just heard, the thing that happened this morning: they must remain secrets, just you and me.'

Zarina nodded gravely.

Samantha's husky voice lowered to a whisper. 'You saved my life. I'll never forget it.'

'Were you frightened? The man was so big, at least ten feet tall, and his shoulders were wider than Nathan's.'

'I was terrified.' She held Zarina's gaze. A child like this — beautiful, bold, intelligent

— could have been hers if her husband had lived. Then she'd have been the wife of the local doctor, the mother of his children, not a killer of men.

'You look awfully sad,' Zarina said. 'Is it those men? Is it because you don't want to be here?'

'It's not the men, and I like being here with you. I was just thinking about someone I lost a long time ago, and something very precious that I've been denied.'

Zarina pondered for a moment, trying to make sense of what Samantha had said. Finding the whole thing too perplexing, she shrugged, and asked, 'Have you discovered where my mummy is?'

'Not yet, but I think I soon will. I went to see the social services people in Beckminster this morning. It seems the woman your mother had the argument with has had a relapse.'

'A relapse?'

'Become ill again. The wounds on her scalp have turned septic. She's back in hospital.'

A satisfied smile curled Zarina's lips. 'When did she get ill again?'

'A couple of days ago, I gather.'

The smile widened until it stretched from ear to ear. 'It was the spell I cast. It worked!'

'Coincidence,' Samantha said.

'I copied the invocations from the grimoire. I did the ritual just as the book said. The magic really does work if you do it right.'

Samantha laughed. 'It was pure coincidence. But if you're so sure it was your spell, you should call a truce now the woman's sick and in pain.'

'She took my brother and sister and mother away. I want her to be sick and in pain. I'm going to do a spell for her to die.' The girl fell silent and her expression became imploring. In a plaintive little voice, she asked, 'If Alexander dies, and Mummy and Amir and Maria don't come back, can I live with you?'

'Come here.'

Zarina climbed off the sofa and ran around the desk. Samantha folded her in her arms. 'Don't talk like that. Don't even think things like that. I'm going to find your mother and bring her home.'

Zarina wriggled free so she could look into Samantha's face. 'When?'

'Soon. It has to be soon.' Turning back to the desk, she gave the gun a final wipe with her cotton-gloved hands, then wedged it into her bag. 'No matter what it costs, no matter what has to be done, I'm going to bring her home.'

'And Amir and Maria?'

'Them too.'

The chunky two-way radio began to hiss. The red channel light was flashing. Samantha lifted it from the desk and pressed a key. The hissing stopped. 'What is it, Charlie?'

'There's a lady at the gate, ma'am. A Mrs Wallace. She says she's the professor's sister, paying a visit.'

'Does she look as if she might be his sister?'

'She looks a good deal younger than him. In her late thirties, early forties, I'd say. I think I can see a family resemblance.'

'Try to keep her out of the house for a while, Charlie. Ask her for some ID.'

'She's very irate, ma'am.'

'Do your best. Chat to her. Try and give me fifteen minutes, then bring her through to the library.'

'I'll try, ma'am. Fifteen minutes.'

Samantha turned to Zarina. 'Alexander's sister's at the gates. A woman called Mrs Wallace.'

Zarina grimaced. 'Aunt Helen. Mrs Mean and Miserable. She hates Mummy. She'll hardly talk to me.'

Samantha rose, took her hand and led her down the long line of display cases towards the door. 'Go and find Nathan for me. Tell him I want him to unfasten the doors of the stable where the big car's being kept, and tell him I'd like him to help me with something tonight, after dark.' They emerged into the passageway. Samantha turned towards the main stairs. Zarina began to run towards the kitchen and the door to the rear yard. 'Stay out of the way,' Samantha called after her. 'Don't come into the house while Mrs Wallace is here. Whatever you do, don't let her see you.'

'Alexander will tell her I'm here.'

'I'll tell her he's hallucinating. Now go,' she urged. 'Go quickly.'

9

There was a gentle tapping. The library door opened and the guard entered, looking bulky and out of place in his blue uniform and heavy boots. He advanced down the room. 'Mrs Wallace, ma'am. She's come to visit her brother. You asked me to bring her to you.' He side-stepped into a gap between the table display cases, then retreated back to the door, glad to be rid of his charge.

Helen Wallace was in full view now. There could be no doubt that she was Alexander's sister. The genes that had given her brother his refined features had worked in her to produce a very pretty woman.

Samantha ran an expert eye over her clothes: stylish suit, probably expensive, but the skirt unfashionably short; a rather fussy blouse, shoes too staid and handbag big and shapeless and black when it should have been navy blue. She moved towards her, smiled and held out a hand. 'It's a pleasure to meet you, Mrs Wallace. My name's Grey; Georgina Grey.' Closer to her now, she could see the woman's cheeks were flushed with anger and the heat of the day.

Helen Wallace ignored the outstretched hand. 'I can't begin to tell you how annoyed I am, Miss Grey,' she seethed. 'To be stopped at the gates of my brother's home, my family home, to be asked by some great oaf of a man to identify myself, to be kept waiting after I've travelled all — '

'You must blame me for that, Mrs Wallace. He was acting on my instructions.' Samantha gave her another radiant smile, then turned and led her towards the leather sofa near Alexander's desk. 'I'm sure you'd like tea after your journey. I've had a tray brought through.'

Something hard pressed against Helen Wallace's thigh when she settled herself on the worn leather. She reached down and pulled out a book. *Anne of Green Gables.* It fell open. Inside the cover her brother had written, *To Zarina with love from Alexander.* Sentimental old fool. He'd allowed the mother and her child to bleed him dry. When something in a skirt walked through the door his brains flew out of the window. She scowled at Samantha. 'Perhaps you could tell me what this is all about?'

'Security, Mrs Wallace. And your brother's medical care. Some weeks ago a friend of his called, found him ill and the house and its contents unprotected. He appointed nurses, arranged for a doctor to visit and for someone to watch over the place.'

'Nurses? How many nurses?'

'Three, for twenty-four-hour cover. And the doctor calls almost daily.'

Helen Wallace took the cup from Samantha. 'And you're in charge of it all, I take it?'

Samantha nodded. 'Milk and sugar?'

'Just a little milk, no sugar. Someone at the council assured me they'd arranged home care.'

Samantha poured milk from a delicate blue and gold china jug. 'It was very basic. He was left alone in the house for much of the time.'

Helen sipped at the hot tea. Thank God. She needed that. She should have stopped off on the way down, had a meal, taken a break. She eyed the elegant young woman over the rim of her cup. Her crimson dress was stylish and rather low cut. God knows what all this must be doing to Alexander: nurses, this glamorous creature. Alexander would respond to her, all right. She rattled her cup down on its saucer. 'I was told by the social services people that they couldn't find him a hospital bed or a place in a hospice.' She flinched when she tried to meet Samantha's gaze. Those eyes! So vivid, so accusing. She sensed criticism, an unspoken accusation of neglect. 'And I have a husband,' she went on, defending herself, 'and teenage children taking exams, and a home of my own to care for. I couldn't just leave everything and rush down here.'

Samantha nodded. 'Of course not. I understand. Biscuit?' She held out a blue and gold plate. Mrs Wallace shook her head. 'More tea?'

She nodded gratefully. 'Please.'

Samantha held the lid of the pot and poured. 'Have you any idea where his wife might have gone?' She added milk.

Helen lifted the second cup to her lips. Her sister-in-law's whereabouts were none of this woman's business, and she'd only start blabbing to Alexander and cause trouble. The least said about Rasha the better. She shrugged. 'She must have decided to jump ship. I can only think she's taken the children back to Egypt. She has family there. Her eldest child wasn't Alexander's. Perhaps she's still in contact with the girl's father; perhaps she's gone back to him.'

The door opened, footsteps approached and Nurse Stockwell appeared, starched skirt rustling faintly. 'The professor's awake now,' she announced. 'He's having one of his good days. Shall I take you up, Mrs Wallace?'

'I think I can find my own way to my brother's room,' Helen Wallace snapped. She rose, rattled her cup and saucer onto the tray, then, bristling with anger, brushed past the nurse.

Josie Stockwell grimaced at Samantha. 'I'll take a break, give her half an hour, then I'll go back up. He's not had all of his medication.'

When the nurse had left, Samantha snatched up Helen's bag, took it over to the desk and began to empty it: a comb, a small silver-backed brush, paper handkerchiefs, a mobile phone. She switched it on, selected Contacts, and scrolled the list of entries displayed on the screen: Howard, High Cross School, some Christian names, Dr Asadi, RAC, Garage, Doctor, Dentist, more Christian names. She switched it off, put it on the desk, then searched deeper in the voluminous bag. A leather purse. She unzipped it, found the usual plethora of plastic cards, banknotes, small change, folded till receipts. She laid the purse beside the phone and continued searching. Cosmetics, pens, a tiny three-days-to-a-page diary. She flicked through to the current day and read, *Alexander, Sourbeck*, and beneath it, *Dr Asadi, 11.30.* A postcode had been heavily underlined.

She leafed through to the address pages. *Mrs Carver, Social Services, Billingham Borough Council*, was listed, as was a *Dr Asadi, Norhope Lodge, Granly:* one of the names on the Contacts list held in the mobile phone. Where was Granly? Samantha copied the details down, then flicked through the diary one last time. *Car service. Dentist. Sports day. Flowers and brasses. WI meeting. Bridge at Mrs Banks:* terse reminders of the events that filled the ordered life of a middle-class housewife.

A rectangle of card dropped onto the desk. Samantha picked it up and read: *Norhope Lodge, Granly. A caring and secure environment for the mentally ill. Dr Karif Asadi, M.B.ChB. M.I.C.P., Consultant Psychiatrist.* Then, beneath a handwritten telephone number: *One of the Rashman-Halim Group of Private Health Care Facilities.* She scribbled down the details, then replaced everything in the bag and took it back to the sofa.

Samantha lowered herself into Alexander's chair, pressed the toe of a crimson shoe against the leg of the desk and swung herself gently to and fro. The social worker had assured her Helen Wallace had been consulted and kept informed, that she'd been told about Alexander's wife. Not only did she know where Rasha was, it would seem she'd paid her a visit less than a couple of hours before arriving here. Why would she withhold what she knew? Why would she suggest Rasha had run away? Perhaps —

The tiny beacon on the radio-phone began to flash. Samantha reached over the desk and keyed it on. 'Yes, Charlie?'

'Man arrived to collect the car, ma'am.'

'You've checked his ID?'

'Yes. He's okay. He's from the Department.'

'Ask him to drive into the rear yard — the gates are open. I'll meet him there.'

When Samantha passed through the kitchen, Mrs Binnington was sitting at the old deal table, peeling potatoes. 'Thanks for bringing tea through, Norma.'

'Dinner's going to be at six. I've got to get away early tonight. Will the visitor be staying?'

'I'm sure she will.'

'I'll peel a couple more. Shall I find her a room and make up a bed?'

'Don't worry about that. Nicole and I can make up a bed and get her anything she needs.' She moved past the battered Welsh dresser and stepped out into the yard. A new-looking Volvo was just turning into the gateway. Nathan had reversed the embassy limousine out of the stable, and Samantha gestured to the driver of the black Volvo to pass through the open doors. As she approached the car a short, stocky man with receding grey hair climbed out and turned towards her. She smiled. 'And you are?'

'Wordsworth, Lakeland Couriers.'

'And I'm Shirley Temple.'

'Nice to meet you, Shirley. Is this it?' He nodded towards the gleaming Daimler.

'That's it. The pennant on the wing's been rolled up and tied. We couldn't get the embassy crest off the grill, but we've stuck silver tape over it.'

He strolled round to the front of the car and settled his hands on his hips. His shirt sleeves were rolled up to the elbows, his collar unfastened, his tie loose, his black trousers tightly belted. 'That's fine.' He grinned across at her. 'Can't beat a bit of gaffer tape. I'll be taking it back to the depot on trade plates.'

'There are four packages, to be given to Marcus Soames personally.' Samantha reached through the driver's window, slid the keys from the ignition, then went to the back of the car and opened the boot.

The man joined her and gazed down at the large brown-paper-wrapped bundles. 'Any documents? The major said there'd be documents.'

'Inside the packages.'

He nodded and slammed the boot lid down. 'And I've got a delivery for you, Shirley.'

'Ulrick gave you the extra items?'

'You just caught me. I was with her when you called.' Samantha followed him round the Volvo and he lifted the hatch. 'Where do you want them?'

'On the bench against the back wall. I'll find somewhere more secure when you've gone.'

He picked up a clipboard and tapped a rough wooden box with his pencil. 'A dozen grenades: six standard and six extended delay. Ulrick said the standard delay is pretty reliable at five seconds; the extendeds seem to vary between fifteen and twenty-five, but they've never had one less than ten.' He grinned at her. 'There's always a first time, I suppose. I won't ask you what they're for.' He studied his clipboard. 'Six hundred rounds for a Heckler sub,' he tapped a waxed canvas bundle, 'and three boxes of red-tipped shells for a semi-automatic. That it?'

'Body bags: I asked for six body bags.'

He nodded. 'On the seat in the back of the car.' He tugged open a door, lifted out the black nylon shrouds and carried them to the back of the stable. He draped them over a rusty iron manger, then returned for the boxes.

'You've been very helpful,' Samantha said. 'Will you have a meal with us before you go?'

He picked up a pair of red trade plates then slammed down the hatch. 'Thanks, but no.' He knelt down and began to fix one over the

Daimler's front licence plate with heavy rubber bands. 'Want to get back. Taking the wife out for a meal. Wedding anniversary.' He covered the plate at the rear, then took a peaked cap and black jacket from the Volvo and brought the clipboard over to her. 'Could you sign the docket for me? Pink copy's yours.'

She scrawled an illegible signature.

He slid his arms into the jacket and fastened his shirt collar. 'Nice place,' he said. 'Very rural. Don't expect you get many callers.'

Samantha smiled as she handed back the board. 'You'd be surprised.'

He straightened his tie then settled the peaked cap over his bald patch. 'Feel a bit like an undertaker's assistant, but I thought I should look as if I went with the car.' He extended a hand. 'Nice meeting you, Shirley.'

'And you.'

He settled himself behind the wheel of the limousine, adjusted the seat, then slammed the door and keyed the ignition. The starter whined. 'Don't forget, never less than ten seconds.'

'Happy anniversary.'

He laughed, touched his cap, then accelerated gently out of the yard.

* * *

Helen Wallace closed the library door and strode on past the show cases, glancing idly at amulets, finger sheaths, fragments of pottery, tiny figurines, as she headed towards the sofa.

Tomb robbings. She sniffed dismissively. Remnants of the long-dead, mementos of her father's and brother's wasted lives. The bits and pieces in here probably weren't worth a lot, she reflected. The really valuable things were in trays in the safe, or in cabinets in the air-conditioned room. She looked into the bay window that accommodated Alexander's desk. The black-haired woman wasn't there, but the tea was still on the table beside the sofa. She sat down and felt the pot. It was barely warm. She topped it up with water from a jug, poured a cup, added milk, drank it thirstily, then poured another and took a couple of biscuits.

She hadn't spent long with Alexander; the nurse coming in had been a welcome excuse to leave. He'd asked her about Howard and the children, asked her why they hadn't come with her. He liked Howard and the children, but there wasn't much love lost between her and Alexander. The truth was, he irritated her. No, he jolly well angered her. Marrying that Egyptian dancer, bringing her and her little love child back to the family home. She simply couldn't bear it if everything passed to them.

The cool silence of the house had calmed her. She could think more clearly now. And there was so much to think about. Alexander might be seriously ill, but he didn't seem close to death, and she couldn't possibly pay what Dr Asadi was asking to confine Rasha in the home indefinitely. If Rasha came out she'd resume her role as wife and mistress of Sourbeck, the children's adoption would fall through and Rasha would inherit everything.

Howard should be helping her with this. He was clever, he'd think of something, but he wasn't interested. In fact, he'd be appalled if he knew what she was trying to do. Highly educated men could be so unworldly and weak. She brushed crumbs from her skirt and rattled her cup down on the tray.

The door clicked, stiletto heels began to thud down the room. She turned. That lipstick, the nails, the dress, the shoes: so much red. Red as blood. She had to admit it suited the woman. It was the crown of black hair that did it; so stylishly cut. And the eyes. Dear God, those eyes.

'You've seen Alexander?' Samantha joined her on the sofa.

Helen nodded. 'He looked much better than I expected.'

'He has good days and bad days.'

'What's the doctor's prognosis?'

'He won't make one.'

'Alexander told me Zarina's here. He said she comes and sits with him most afternoons.'

'He's hallucinating. The doctor's prescribed diamorphine to control the pain; it leaves him confused and gives him terrible dreams.'

Mrs Wallace gave Samantha a questioning look. 'Dreams?'

'Mostly about his wife being sexually assaulted.'

'He said you'd overpowered an intruder and dragged him out at gunpoint.'

Samantha smiled. 'Dreams,' she repeated. 'He can't distinguish dreams from reality.' They eyed one another down the length of the sofa. Presently, Samantha said, 'I hope you'll dine with us and stay the night?'

'I don't think so, Miss Grey. Alexander is being very well cared for and you seem to have everything under control; there's nothing I can do. I'd be in the way.'

'Rasha's gone, he's lost his children. He'd be greatly comforted by your being here.'

Helen Wallace laughed. 'We don't have a

lot to say to one another, Miss Grey. In fact, we've never really hit if off since we were children. He'll take much more comfort from having you and the nurses fussing around him.'

'Dinner's at six. Surely you'll have a meal with us before you go?'

'I'd rather start the journey; get as far as I can while it's light.' She reached for her bag then rose to her feet. 'But I would like to take a shower, freshen up before I set off. It was so hot driving down.'

'No one's using the bathroom. Plenty of clean towels in the airing cupboard.'

Helen moved towards the door. 'I'll just get my things from the car.' When she as halfway down the room she turned and looked back. 'I presume the store where Alexander keeps his collection is secure?'

'It's kept locked. Nathan checks the air-conditioning twice a week. Apart from that, no one goes in.'

Helen rolled her eyes heavenwards. 'The deaf mute! One of the maids was married to the head gardener; he was their child. I expected Alexander to get rid of him when Father died, but he kept him on.'

'Why wouldn't he keep him on?'

'Well, for one thing he certainly doesn't improve the tone of the place. And deaf and dumb's bad enough, but he's like something out of a horror film.'

'We think he's rather sweet.'

'We?'

'The nurses, the housekeeper, me.'

'Sweet's the very last word I'd use. Does he still live in that vile little bothy across the yard?'

Samantha nodded. 'But he's started having his evening meal with us in the kitchen.'

Mrs Wallace grimaced. 'How can you possibly bear it? Nathan in the house? Mummy would never have allowed it. She used to shoo him away from the kitchen door when he was a child. She must be turning in her grave.'

When Helen had left the room, Samantha went behind the desk, found her encrypted mobile, and keyed in a number.

Almost immediately, a male voice announced, 'Selfridges Department Store.'

'Put me through to Judy Garland in fine china and glassware.'

'It's Shirley,' the man said. 'Shirley Temple.'

'How did you guess?'

'It's the sexy voice. It's unforgettable. One moment.'

Samantha listened to the hiss in the earpiece, the faint clicks as the encryption changed. Suddenly, out of the silence, a female voice asked, 'How can I help you, Miss Temple?'

Samantha flicked through to the page in her notebook. 'A Doctor Karif Asadi: he's the consultant psychiatrist at a place called Norhope Lodge, Granly. I'd like you to check him out, find out what you can about him.'

'Will do. Do you know anything about him, his nationality, anything to give us a lead?'

'Not a thing.'

'No worries. I'll check the name against the database and take it from there.'

'How soon can you get back to me?'

'Depends how the search through the system goes.'

'By 8 a.m. tomorrow?'

'Someone will call you and give you whatever we've found. I'm going off in an hour, but I'll set things in motion and ask them to get back to you.'

'There are two others.'

'Go ahead. I'm listening.'

'A Dr Reginald Suttcliffe. He's the director of social services at Billingham Borough Council. And a Mrs Brenda Carver. She's the head of the child welfare section there. Find out what you can: private addresses, telephone records over the past six months, details of immediate family and friends, bank statements covering the past year if you can.'

'That's going to take a little longer.'

'Give it your best shot.'

'That it?'

'For now.'

'If we find something on Asadi, do you want calling during the night?'

'Anything interesting, just call me.' Samantha dropped the encrypted phone into her bag.

* * *

Helen Wallace studied her reflection in the mirror. She was working on her hair, trying to restore some of the wave and curl, some of the bounce the rollers had given it before she'd left home that morning. God, what a day! The long, hot, sticky drive down; Dr Asadi's outrageous proposal. She still couldn't believe it, for all sorts of reasons. He was a doctor, for heaven's sake, and she was a mature woman with teenage children. She gave up on her hair, dipped the tip of her little finger into a tiny jar, and began to shade the skin above her eyes, winking at herself as she worked the brownish-blue paste over the lids.

Rasha had revamped the bathroom. New bath, enclosed shower, huge basin, toilet, bidet, wall-to-ceiling mosaic tiles. The presence of women in the house was obvious: black tights — presumably the nurses' — draped over the radiator; bottles and jars ranged along the rim of the bath, the basin, the window sill. She'd helped herself. She felt fragrant again after the cool shower and a change of underwear.

With deft upward strokes of a tiny brush, she applied mascara. Not her own; some expensive lash-lengthening stuff she'd found on the shelf beneath the mirror. It did something, no doubt about that, and the face powder had cooled the pinkness of her cheeks and chin.

She slid the brush back in the tube, sat on the rim of the bath and rummaged in her bag for her mobile phone. She pressed keys. If he says something nice to me, if he asks me to come home, I will. The ringing stopped and a man's voice recited the number.

'That you, Howard?'

'Helen. You've arrived then? You okay?'

'I'm so-so, Howard, just so-so.'

'How was the drive down?'

'Long, hot and tiring, and when I got here I found the place overrun with strangers: nurses, a housekeeper, men minding the gates,' she lowered her voice, 'and a strange-looking woman in charge of it all.'

'Strange?'

'A mop of black hair with a fringe, beautifully cut and styled; she looked a bit like those women in Egyptian tomb paintings. And she had big scary eyes. I'll talk to you about her later.'

'I can't wait. How's old Alexander?'

'Surprisingly healthy. He was clean and tidy and sitting in his dressing gown by the bed when I saw him. He's being looked after extremely well.'

'Good for him. You must have enjoyed the chat. It's been a long time.'

'Can't say that I did, Howard. You know we've never been close. He asked after you and the children.' She made her voice accusing. 'He wanted to know why you hadn't come down.'

'Harriet and Tim are relaxing after exams and I'm working and rehearsing. I hope you explained. What about Rasha?'

'Still in the psychiatric hospital.' Quickly changing the subject, she asked, 'How are you, Howard?'

'Fine; everything's fine. Results came through from the Examination Board. My girls have done awfully well.'

'That's nice for you, Howard. Are you managing?' *Please say you're missing me. At least say something nice to me.*

'Managing?'

'At home — you and the children?'

'We're fine. I'm just catching up on some marking; they're watching television. We're going into town for an Italian later, then I'm taking them along to watch rehearsals. Play's starting to take shape. Veronica Upton's perfect as Linton's sister.'

Long blonde hair, pretty face, emphatic breasts — probably implants — no wonder Howard sounded enthusiastic. He was so wrapped up in his own little world, so completely indifferent to her. *Say you love me, damn you. Say you're missing me. At least ask me how I am and sound as if you're interested.*

She lowered her voice, softened it, and asked, 'Would you like me to come home?'

'Come home?' He sounded surprised. 'You've only just got there. Thought you were staying for a few days?'

'I could come home if you'd like me to, Howard. Alexander's being well cared for.' She felt a prickling behind her eyes. How many more times did she have to drop the hint? He was so clever, yet so stupid and insensitive when it came to the things that really mattered. He had the emotional intelligence of a 5-year-old. At least he could have asked her if anything was wrong. It was like talking to a lump of wood. 'Would you like me to?'

'Like you to what?'

'Come home.'

'It's close on two hundred miles, Helen. And you've not seen Alex for ages. It could be the last time.'

Her heart sank. 'I suppose you're right. I'll call you again tomorrow. Whatever you do, don't call me on the house phone. If there's an emergency, call me on my mobile.'

'Bit difficult, is it? I'd better let you call me . . . '

Helen closed her eyes. *Say you love me. Say you love me. For God's sake, say you love me. I need you to say it, Howard.*

' . . . And take care, Helen. See you later in the week. Bye.' The phone clicked and went dead.

She'd tried her very best. It was all his stupid fault. Taking a deep breath, she reached into her bag, found her diary and plucked out the square of white card. Then, hands shaking, stomach churning, she keyed the handwritten number into her mobile.

10

The sound of footsteps, the chink of bottles and jars on the metal trolley, came faintly through the connecting door. The night nurse was making sure Alexander was comfortable before returning to her chair beside the bed. Samantha had taken what had once been a dressing room adjoining the master bedroom. She had to be close to him, this man she'd been assigned to protect, whose secrets she'd been ordered to discover.

Events of the past few days, things Zarina had told her, had convinced her that intruders might be lurking in the woods surrounding the house; watching and waiting. She'd given instructions for shutters to be swung across the ground-floor windows after dark, their iron locking bars dropped into place. On the first floor, curtains had to be drawn before lights were switched on.

A guard patrolled the outside of the house and the gated rear yard. Tomorrow she'd go up to the attic, out onto the roof, and check the view from the parapets. The encroaching trees would limit its usefulness as a vantage point, but shots could be fired, or grenades thrown down, in an emergency. Marcus could be callous and uncaring. He should have granted her request for more guards. Three weren't enough to patrol and protect the house and grounds.

The heat of the day had lingered in the upper rooms, making it too hot for sleep. Samantha stood by her open window, gazing across the moonlit forecourt, watching for movement amongst the shadows beneath the trees. A fox, long-legged and rangy, sidled out on to the paving, stared towards the house, then lowered its head and began to wander around, sniffing. Suddenly it cocked its ears and listened to the night before turning and loping back into the darkness of the wood.

Her entire body was aching. She hadn't wanted to involve the guards — there were things best hidden from them — and she'd had to call on Nathan. It would have been impossible without his help. Dog-like in his devotion, he saw no reason to question her authority. Deaf to sound, incapable of speech, he seemed to have a heightened awareness of things. He understood, without explanation, why she was here: the mistress and the children had been taken away; his master was ill and vulnerable. A glance, a gesture, were all the instruction he required. He seemed to know instinctively what had to be done, and he did it willingly.

She'd taken him to the corpses of the men she'd killed that afternoon: one beside the overgrown track; the other in the abandoned office. He'd helped her zip them into body bags, then he'd dragged the bags to the rim of the quarry and loaded them with stones before sliding them over the edge. It was a long drop. There'd been quite a wait before the splash when they hit the pool.

While she'd held a lamp, he'd secured the shutter in the office. One of the guards had already collected the car from beneath the dead tree, driven it round to the stable block and parked it beside the courier's Volvo. Tomorrow, she'd search it; give some thought to disposing of it. And she might —

The door behind her clicked open. Samantha turned. Wide and troubled eyes were gazing at her around its edge. A small voice whispered, 'I've woken up and I can't get back to sleep, Georgie.'

'Come and sit on the bed. Don't make a sound. We don't want to disturb Alexander.'

Zarina scampered across the moonlit room, climbed up on the bed and sat, cross-legged, in her pink pyjamas. 'I can't stop thinking about Mummy and Maria and Amir.' Her voice was tearful.

Samantha left the window, sat beside the

child and slid an arm around her. She drew her close. 'Try not to worry. I'm going to bring them home.'

'When?'

'Soon.'

'Tomorrow?'

'Perhaps not tomorrow, but soon.'

Zarina had a child's unquestioning trust. The words reassured her, and she immediately turned her thoughts to less distressing things. 'That's a pretty nightdress. And you smell nice.'

Samantha smiled. 'It's a perfume called Mitsouko. Would you like some?' She reached for a tiny bottle, applied some to her finger and dabbed it behind Zarina's ears and on her wrists. She stoppered the bottle and slid it back onto her bedside table.

Zarina sniffed at her wrists, then whispered, 'Do you have a boyfriend?' She lifted her wrist to her nose again.

'My very best friend — my very best friend after you — is a man, so yes, I suppose I do have a boyfriend.'

'Does he kiss you?'

'Sometimes I kiss him on the cheek.'

'But he doesn't kiss you?'

Samantha shook her head.

'Don't you let him? Isn't he a very good kisser?'

Samantha laughed softly. 'I should think he'd be a very good kisser.'

'If he's your boy friend, and he doesn't kiss you, what does he do?'

'Mmm . . . He cares for me.'

'Cares for you?'

'Fixes my hair, washes my clothes, takes suits and dresses to the cleaners, keeps the house clean and tidy. Sometimes he cooks me special meals. And we go away on holiday together.'

'Where on holiday?'

'Mostly Europe: places in France, Italy, Spain. He helps me choose clothes. He has a great sense of style; an eye for colour.'

'Does he stroke your bottom?' Seeing the surprised look on Samantha's face, Zarina added hastily, 'Alexander used to stroke Mummy's bottom. She'd laugh and lift his hand up to her waist and say, 'Later, Alex, later.''

'I'd be rather surprised if he stroked my bottom.'

They gazed at one another, their faces lit by moonlight. A faint breeze made the net curtains ripple. In the woods beyond the forecourt a fox barked, a startled owl hooted.

Clearly perplexed, Zarina abandoned the intimate questions and moved on to safer ground. 'What's his name?'

'Crispin.'

'Have you got a photograph of him?'

Samantha shook her head. The girl looked disappointed, so she added, 'But I know where we can find one.' She held her finger to her lips, rose from the bed and gently opened the connecting door. She peered into Alexander's bedroom. The nurse was dozing. Alexander appeared to be in a deep, drug-induced sleep. A small table lamp illuminated a book lying open on the nurse's lap. Samantha whispered, 'Go over to the pile of magazines on the table by Nicole's chair and bring a few back. Be very quiet. She'll be startled if you wake her up.'

Zarina crept off and, with an exaggerated display of stealth, returned with an armful of fashion magazines and colour supplements from the Sunday papers. She climbed up on the bed. Samantha drew the curtains, switched on the bedside lamp and sat beside her. She flicked through one of the magazines, then another. Presently she found the page she was looking for and handed the magazine to Zarina.

'Gosh!' she whispered. 'Awesome. Better than a film star.' She looked up. 'This is Crispin? This is your boy friend?'

Samantha nodded.

Zarina studied the full-page black-and-white image. Hooded eyes gazed back at her out of an unsmiling and darkly handsome face. Crispin had been artfully lit by the photographer. His features, the contours of his arms, his torso, the skimpy pants stretched tight over muscular thighs, were defined by deep shadows.

'Who are Donchi and Giordano?'

'People who make luxurious and incredibly expensive things. They use Crispin's picture to make their advertisement eye-catching.'

'Is his picture in magazines a lot?'

'Not quite so often now. He's becoming just a little too old.'

'He doesn't look old.'

'They seem to prefer very young — '

The encrypted phone began to bleep. Samantha snatched it from the bedside table and keyed it on. A woman demanded, 'Who's there?'

'Shirley; Shirley Temple. What have you got for me?'

'We've searched the database. The only Dr Asadi we could find is listed as dead. He was the consultant psychiatrist in charge of a mental hospital in Northern Iraq. When the Americans reached the place after the invasion they found it in the hands of a few orderlies and couple of nurses. It was pretty chaotic; patients weren't being properly fed or medicated. The doctor who assisted Asadi had gone to Baghdad to see if family members had survived the bombing; the chief nurse had vanished.

'The Americans didn't want a repeat of the fiasco at the Baghdad hospital where rioters and looters broke in, so they allocated some of their own people to run the place while they tried to locate the staff. They were told that Dr Asadi had dismissed the chief nurse following allegations of sexual assault on female patients; he'd only had the job a few months. When Asadi checked with other hospitals they all reported similar incidents.

'Asadi was found dead on the outskirts of Mosul a few days later; he'd been beaten and strangled. The chief nurse was called Nuwaf Al-Museck. The Americans put him on their wanted list, but he was never found. They didn't give it a very high priority.'

'Got any pictures?'

'A good one of Dr Asadi and a grainy blow-up of an ID photograph worn by the nurse. The Americans got it from a hospital where he'd worked previously. It's not recent. And there are copies of some reports the Americans prepared, and copies of correspondence with the Iraqi authorities. It's all pretty much as I've said, but there's personal information on Asadi and Museck. Got your laptop handy? We could do a download.'

'It's here.' Samantha rose from the bed and crossed over to a dressing table. 'I'm just booting it up.' She took a cable from a pocket in the laptop's carrying case, connected the encrypted phone, then cleared the logos from the computer screen. 'I'm ready. Send it.'

'Will do. Are you okay now — about Dr Asadi, I mean? I don't think we're going to find anything else.'

'That's fine. I'm grateful. Is someone working on the other two names?'

'I've left a note for the people on the morning shift. You should have something by the end of the day.' A click in the earpiece was followed by a burring drone as the data began to come through.

Samantha turned to Zarina. 'Bed! It's after two o'clock.'

'Can I stay with you?' The child was begging her with her eyes.

'Just this once. Take the side furthest from the door.'

'There's a man's face coming on the screen. Who is it?'

Samantha slid her hand beneath the pillows and made sure the gun was on her side of the bed. 'Just a man I'm trying to trace. Now, go to sleep,' she whispered, and switched off the lamp.

* * *

The narrow country road wound through undulating countryside. Samantha braked gently, rounded a bend, then cruised past a row of cottages, a village shop, an old Saxon church with a crenellated tower, a couple of mean-looking bungalows. Pavements ended, then grass verges and low stone walls bordered the road. After another mile she saw the sign behind spear-topped railings: *Norhope Lodge, Secure Psychiatric Hospital.* She allowed the car to roll to a stop and looked through a gateway at a Victorian house of considerable size. Dormers punctuated a steeply sloping roof of blue slate. A dozen tall windows, rectangles of darkness enclosed by grimy red brickwork, were arranged symmetrically around a pillared entrance.

She'd made the forty-mile journey from Sourbeck in the big Volvo left at the Hall by the courier. The low-slung Ferrari with its confined cab wouldn't be suitable for a passenger who might be drugged and difficult to move. And Rasha had to be taken home today. She couldn't spend any more time on this.

While the engine whispered, she took a last look at the images the research team had sent her. Dr Karif Asadi had been bald, round-faced, stocky, and looked to be moving into late middle age. Nuwaf Al-Museck, the male nurse he'd dismissed, was dark-eyed with curly black hair and a short, neatly trimmed beard. The photograph had probably been taken when he was in his early thirties. He'd be around forty now. She folded the images, put them back in her bag, then let out the clutch. The black saloon passed through the gateway and swept on down a tarmac drive that curved across a couple of acres of well-tended lawn.

The entrance door was locked. *Press for Reception* was engraved beneath a button on a bright metal box attached to one of the architraves. She pressed. Seconds later a female voice chirped, 'Reception. How can I help you?'

'I'd like to speak to Dr Asadi.'

'You have an appointment?'

'No, but I need to talk to him about placing a relative here. It's rather urgent.'

'Mr Brisling, our head of administration, could deal with that for you. Would — '

'There are problems; medical problems. I have to talk to the consultant in charge before I can make a decision.'

'This would be a private placement?'

'That's correct.'

'May I have your name?'

'Grey; Georgina Grey.'

'I'm going to release the lock, Miss Grey. Please step inside.'

A mechanism clicked. Samantha turned the handle, the door opened and she passed through a glass lobby into a large entrance hall. On her left, a broad stairway curved up to the first floor. On her right, the word *RECEPTION* had been etched into the upper panel of a half-glazed door. A white-haired woman emerged.

'Dr Asadi is on the wards, Miss Grey. If you wouldn't mind taking a seat for a moment, I'll locate him and tell him you're here.' She gestured towards a low table and a couple of chairs. 'I can't promise he'll see you right away. If he's involved with a patient he could be a little while.' She smiled, then, white cotton blouse straining across her shoulders, blue skirt tight across broad hips, returned to her office.

Samantha glanced at the magazines laid out on the table in neat rows, then moved a chair aside so she could study the oak-framed photographs arranged along the wall behind it. One held her attention. A strip of card, fixed beneath the glass, was inscribed, *Dr Karif Asadi, M.B.ChB, M.I.C.P., Consultant Psychiatrist.* Dark suit instead of nurse's overalls, youthful face fleshed out by maturity, beard neatly trimmed, it was Nuwaf Al-Museck, the man the real Dr Asadi had dismissed.

It was as she'd expected. She reached beneath her jacket, released the strap that held the gun in its shoulder holster and thumbed over the safety catch. Marcus had instructed her not to involve the Department in any search for Alexander's wife and children, but she had to intimidate the man, quickly coerce him into doing what she wanted. And she needed him to remain here, available to talk to the authorities, to answer any questions about the decision he was going to have to make. She'd show him her ID cards, scare him, take control of the situation, then make her demands.

The skirt of her white linen suit was tight, the jacket loose to conceal the shoulder-holster. Black silk blouse, black silk handkerchief bursting out of her top pocket, opaque black stockings, black and white Gucci bag and shoes: it was all a bit thirties retro, but she was running short of clothes. She'd been away from home and Crispin's ministrations for too long.

The white-haired woman appeared through a different doorway at the far end of the hall. 'Dr Asadi will see you now, Miss Grey. If you'll step this way.'

Samantha strode over, followed the woman through a tiny lobby and emerged into a spacious consulting room.

'Miss Grey, Doctor,' the woman announced, then retreated, closing doors behind her.

Samantha glanced around, took in an examination couch, a metal trolley, a window on to a light well; her eyes came to rest on the tall bearded man behind the desk.

He smiled and gestured towards the visitor's chair. 'Please, Miss Grey, sit down, and tell me how I can help you.'

Samantha settled back in the leather chair. 'I'd like to see Dr Karif Asadi.'

The man raised a questioning eyebrow. Using both hands, he gestured towards himself as he said, 'I am Dr Asadi.' His white medical coat was open, revealing the waist-coat of a dark-grey suit. An expensive-looking pen and a bright metal examination torch were protruding from one of the pockets and a stethoscope was clipped around his neck. Another encouraging smile, then he repeated, 'How can I help you, Miss Grey?'

Samantha slid her hand beneath her jacket, wrapped her fingers around the butt of the gun and returned his smile. 'You don't seem to know who you are, Nuwaf. You're Nuwaf Al-Museck, not Karif Asadi.'

His body stiffened, his smile faded, fear

clouded his dark eyes. 'You are quite mistaken. I assure you, I am Dr Karif Asadi.'

Samantha clicked open her bag, took out the image of Dr Asadi and tossed it on the desk.

He snatched it up, unfolded it and scowled at the photograph. Hands shaking now, he glanced back at her and gave the paper a dismissive tap. 'You are mistaken.' His voice was hard and menacing. 'For the third and last time, I am Dr Karif Asadi. And I'd like you to tell me what you mean by tricking your way into my consulting room and saying these preposterous things.'

Samantha reached into her bag again and took out the second photograph. 'I think that's your picture, Nuwaf, and it's your name under the wanted notice. It was posted in every government building, every police station, in Iraq.'

He stared down at the grainy image of his own bearded face, then glared across at her. 'Who are you?'

Samantha took her ID wallet from her bag and reached over the desk so he could read the *Serious Crime Unit* card. Closer to him now, she detected an astringent, citrus-like fragrance: oil of bergamot, she decided, the perfume in the pomade he used on his hair and beard and the pencil-line moustache that curved around his mouth.

'What do you want with me?' he demanded. 'What are your intentions?' Agitated now, he rose to his feet and leaned towards her, his shoulders hunched, his posture menacing.

Samantha pushed her chair back, drew the gun and levelled it. 'We can play this one of two ways, Nuwaf. Either you do something for me, and do it exactly as I say, or I arrest you for the murder of Dr Asadi, the sexual assault of female patients and impersonating a doctor. I think you'd better sit down while we talk about it.'

He scowled at her across the desk, then slowly lowered himself into his chair. 'It was lies,' he muttered. 'Asadi was jealous of me, of the way the patients liked me, of my experience and competence, of my greater knowledge of things. He wanted to get rid of me. He fabricated the charges. I would never harm a patient. I would never abuse a woman.'

'So, you killed him and stole his identity?'

'It was a time of unrest. The country had been invaded; it was lawless. He was a Sunni. He was stupid enough to drive into the Shia area of the town. He was killed by Shia militia. I was shocked to hear of his death. But yes, I did take his papers, his diplomas. I assumed his identity.' His voice became plaintive. 'I lived in difficult times. We were all trying to survive as best we could.'

Samantha held him in an unblinking stare, her face impassive.

'You don't believe me?' he demanded.

'Not a word, Nuwaf. Would you like to hear what I want you to do?'

Angry eyes continued to glare at her. His mouth was hard, his body tense. Presently he gave a resigned sigh; he'd grasped the reality of the situation. 'Tell me,' he muttered. 'Tell me what it is that you want me to do.'

'You have a patient here, a Mrs Rasha Meyer. I want you to release her to me. I want to take her away, this morning.'

'She's been sectioned. She assaulted public officials and the police. She's under heavy sedation. She's not fit to be — '

'She'd just learned her husband was dying, they came to her home and said they were taking her children away. Most women would have reacted in the way she did. I'm not leaving without her, Nuwaf. And you're going to complete the documentation authorizing her release, and write a covering letter for the social services people.'

'It was the police who arranged for her to be sectioned, not the — '

'Stop interrupting and listen to me. I want

her children back. They're in care. I need a letter that social services daren't ignore.' She gestured with the gun. 'Get your pen and a pad. I'm going to tell you what has to be said.'

'Could I remind you that I am the doctor here,' he snapped. 'I decide — '

'You're a psychiatric nurse, Nuwaf, a depraved psychiatric nurse who rapes his female patients. You're no more a doctor than I am. Do you want to do it this way, or do I expose you?'

'How can I trust you? How do I know you won't betray me when I've done what you want?'

'Because I need you here, pretending to be a doctor. I need you to answer questions when they're asked, to explain why you've decided to release her; why her children must be returned. Right now my only concern is to get Rasha Meyer back to her husband and have her children brought home. If you're arrested and charged, or if you disappear, the authorities might question her release.'

'I do this, and I stay here? Nothing will change? Everything will remain as it is?'

'Precisely. Just say in the letter that her condition was an understandable response to extreme stress, that she's responded well to rest and medication, that she no longer presents any risk to her family or the community and that it's imperative that her children be restored to her at the earliest possible time. Then I want you to say that your conversations with her have revealed an unfortunate misunderstanding regarding the suspected abuse of her eldest child. Say Rasha revealed to you that the child experienced abuse at the hands of her great-uncle in Egypt, that since her mother's marriage to Professor Meyer she's been safe and protected, happy in a loving family environment. Wrap it all in the kind of jargon you use.'

He drew a pad of paper onto the blotter and uncapped his pen. 'Just run through those points again while I — '

'Sure, but first of all, call through to the ward and tell them to get her ready to leave. And tell them to put her notes and medicines in a bag so she can take them with her.'

'They need to be administered by someone with knowledge and experience, they — '

'There are nurses in the house, giving round-the-clock care to her husband. A doctor calls every other day. They can deal with it. And you can mention that in the letter as another reason why you saw no problems in letting her go.'

* * *

Rasha Meyer tried to make her eyes focus on the worried faces, vacant faces, grinning faces of the men and women sitting opposite her on the far side of the ward. The morning sun had crept around the corner of the building and the bars on the tall windows were casting hard black shadows across the blue and yellow speckled plastic floor. Maisie, grey hair lank, toothless mouth hanging open, was waving her hand to and fro, shuffling from one canvas-slippered foot to the other, doing her perpetual dance.

Rasha tried to make herself more comfortable on the hard chair. They'd put a fish tank against the wall. A tall cylindrical thing, brightly lit, where tiny fish swam up and down a column of bubbles: contained, imprisoned, their endless movements as futile as Maisie's dance. She was sure the tank was new. She didn't remember it being there yesterday. And perhaps there were a couple of different faces staring back at her from the far side of the room.

Her mind began to feel a little clearer about this time: the time after breakfast, the time before she was given the tablets and the first of her bitter lemon-tasting drinks. After that, things became dreamy again. Things were mostly dreamy. At night, after she'd been taken to her room, she had dark dreams she didn't like, and there was sometimes a fragrance that reminded her of orange peel. Perhaps it was the lingering smell of the stuff they gave her to drink after her evening meal. Thinking about it was beginning to disturb her, but she couldn't imagine why. And other thoughts were trying to come now. Were they memories, or things she'd imagined, things she'd dreamed or read about in magazines? Someone seemed to be calling names to her through a mist: Zarina, Alexander, Amir, Maria. Who were they? If her head would just clear a little more, if the fog would go away, she felt sure she'd know what they all meant to her . . .

There was a rattling of wheels. A nurse in white trousers and a half-sleeved white jacket was pushing a trolley down the room. She paused by each of the inmates, gave them pills to swallow and a tiny plastic beaker of the bitter stuff to drink. To some she said, 'Open your mouth. Open it. Come on, open it.' Then she dropped the brightly coloured pills inside and pressed the plastic beaker against their lips before they could spit them out.

Rasha sighed. Soon she'd be drowsy again. Everything would be sunshine and hazy. No more trying to think about names; no more scary dreams. The trolley rattled to a stop beside her. The nurse gathered up tablets and a beaker, then paused and flicked through papers on a pad. She put the beaker back on the trolley, scattered the tablets in their little trays. 'Nothing for you this morning, Rasha. I wonder what they've got in store for you today?' The nurse laughed and pushed her trolley on to the next patient.

The fish swam up and down the column of bubbles. Maisie had abandoned her shuffling dance and was sitting, legs wide apart, on one of the blue plastic chairs. The sun began to shine into Rasha's eyes. She blinked against the glare, felt a hand touch her arm and glanced up. It was the nurse with the black face and big smile, the one who was gentle when she washed her, the one who stood with her back to her, hiding her, when she sat on the toilet in the cubicles without doors. She was smiling at her now; a big white beam of a smile.

'Rasha? You awake, Rasha? You goin' home, girl. I got to get you washed and dressed, got to get you all smartened up.' She laughed: 'Heh, heh, heh. Got to get you ready to go out on the town.'

* * *

Rasha stared down at her dress. It was yellow, saffron yellow, and the skirt was splattered with what looked like blood. Her sandals were uncomfortable. The straps were cutting into her ankles and toes, and she felt unsteady on the high heels.

'You're goin' to be just fine, honey. And we're goin' to miss you. You been one of my best girls.' The little black nurse laughed. She was always laughing. 'You never given me no trouble.'

They paused by a heavy, iron-barred door. The nurse released her arm, keyed numbers into a pad, then slid it aside. When they'd passed through, she crashed it shut, opened another door, and they moved out across a green-carpeted hall where stairs with a gleaming brass handrail swept up in a great curve. The nurse steered her through a tiny glass vestibule, keyed numbers into another pad, and they stepped out beneath a shallow porch.

A warm breeze touched Rasha's cheek and ruffled her skirt. She inhaled the scent of freshly mown grass, then suddenly tensed. Beyond the steps, across a strip of tarmac, stood a car, and beside it a woman dressed in white linen and black silk; a woman with night-black hair and crimson lips. She felt a stab of alarm. Big black cars and purposeful-looking women made her sense danger. She tried to concentrate her thoughts, tried to remember what it was that was dangerous. When the nurse attempted to lead her down the steps, she resisted.

'Don't be scared, honey. You're going to be fine. Being outside, being in the open, is a bit strange for you, that's all.' The nurse released her arm and handed the woman a carrier bag. 'Medicines, medical notes, records: they're all in there. And a few personal things.' She gave Rasha a hug as she whispered. 'Bye, honey. We're all goin' to miss you,' then she turned and headed back up the steps.

The black-haired woman with crimson lips was studying her intently, a troubled but gentle expression on her face. Rasha suddenly realized she was speaking to her. She tried to concentrate, to understand. 'I'm Georgina,' the soft husky voice was saying. 'I'm going to take you home to Alexander.' The sound of the words, spoken so gently in Arabic, was immensely comforting.

'Home?' Rasha's fear was ebbing away, but she still felt bewildered. She gazed into the woman's eyes, so big and calm and still, and tried to make sense of what she'd said. 'Home, to Egypt, to Mummy and Uncle Asheya? But they live in Cairo, not Alexandria.'

Samantha reached out and took Rasha's hand. Her face was damp with perspiration, the flesh around her eyes puffy, her gaze vacant, her lips wet and trembling. How could they have done this to her? She said gently, 'Home, to Sourbeck Hall, to your husband Alexander and your daughter, Zarina.'

'Husband . . . daughter?'

Samantha opened the passenger door, tossed the carrier bag into the back, then helped her into her seat.

Rasha closed her eyes, unable to keep them open any longer. Her limbs were heavy and her entire being was consumed by an unutterable weariness. She felt a band being draw across her chest, felt hair brushing her cheek, inhaled its fragrance, heard the click of metal on metal. Car doors slammed, something whined, an engine began to murmur; she felt a gentle motion and heard the rumble of tyres on tarmac. Struggling against the encroaching darkness, she forced her eyes open. Shrubs and trees were rushing past. She turned her head. Who was this woman with the black hair and soft husky voice? She felt a warm hand squeezing hers and, as if from a great distance, heard the voice saying, 'He'll pay for this. I promise you, Rasha, I'm going to make the evil bastard pay for this.'

11

Frowns and grimaces drifted over Alexander's face like turbulent clouds chasing one another across a troubled sky. His breathing was rapid and shallow; his trembling lips were shaping words, but the only sounds he uttered were anguished moans.

Samantha sat on the bed, gazing down at the dreaming man. His cheeks were pallid, the flesh on his neck loose and scrawny, but he looked no worse than he had when she'd first arrived; if anything, his appearance had improved. The doctor and nurses were doing their jobs well, but no matter how hard they tried they couldn't hold back the inexorable advance of the enemy within. Sooner or later his body would display that jaundiced yellowing. Then his time would be measured in days.

A scowl furrowed his brow, a grimace dragged down the corners of his mouth, then tired grey eyes blinked open. 'Georgina,' he breathed.

She reached for his hand. It was cold and clammy. 'You've been dreaming, Alexander.'

He closed his eyes again; sucked his cheeks

to moisten his mouth, then whispered, 'Such vile dreams. Utterly grotesque. And always the same; always men being intimate with my wife, and she so accommodating, and so contemptuous and dismissive when I protest.' Suddenly remembering, he beamed up at her. 'But you've found her; you've found Rasha. Zarina brought her in to me.' His voice became distressed. 'She didn't recognize me. Have I changed so much?'

'You've not changed. She's been very heavily sedated. She hasn't recognized Zarina yet. The doctor said two days, maybe three, then her mind will begin to clear.'

'Where did you find her?'

'She was being held in a private psychiatric hospital about thirty miles beyond Beckminster.'

Alexander frowned. He vaguely remembered Samantha telling him something about this but the details eluded him, and thinking about it was too exhausting. Rasha was home; that was all that mattered. He smiled up at Samantha. 'Thank you,' he whispered. 'Thank you for bringing her back to me.'

She squeezed his hand. 'I have to talk to you about something important. I have to ask you to think about leaving.'

'Leaving this life, or leaving the house?'

'The house, of course. You're in danger

here. Ruthless men see you as a threat, and they know you're at Sourbeck.'

'I'd be in danger anywhere.'

'Sourbeck Hall is isolated; difficult to patrol. Rent a house somewhere, or go and stay with your sister for a while. Make it difficult for them to find you.'

'Stay with my sister?' His wheezy laugh turned into a fit of coughing. 'She came to see me,' he spluttered. 'A day ago, a week ago; I can't remember.'

'It was three days ago.'

'Whatever it was, she didn't have much to say; just wanted to know why you and the nurses were here and who was paying for it all. Didn't mention Rasha and the children. We've never really hit it off. She's rather narrow-minded and puritanical, a bit churchy: cleans brasses, arranges flowers on altars, that sort of thing. Loathes Rasha. She didn't visit very often and when she did she hardly spoke to her or the children.'

'Rent a house, then. I'd sort it out for you. We'd spirit you away during the night.'

Tired old eyes studied hers. 'What are you really afraid of?'

'I've already told you, there are people out there who want you dead; some of them desperate to discover what you know before they kill you. I can't guarantee that we'll go on catching intruders; the grounds are too big for the guards to patrol, the house can't be made secure.'

'Intruders? You mean the man who came up here?'

'Him and others.'

'Others? You chased them away?'

'They won't be troubling us any more.'

'You killed them?' he asked, in a shocked little whisper. Bushy eyebrows lifted.

Ignoring his question, she went on: 'I think these people may be getting ready to make a serious assault on the house. This is no place for Rasha and Zarina, and I certainly wouldn't want to bring Amir and Maria back here.'

'I'm dying, Georgina. How long have I got? A few days, a week, a month? The doctor says weeks, but that probably means days. I'm not going to leave Sourbeck.' He sagged back into the pillows and released her hand. 'Would you do something for me?'

'Of course.'

He gestured towards an old mahogany tallboy standing in the shadows beyond the window. 'The first wide drawer beneath the small ones; there's an envelope and a case at the back, hidden behind clothes. Would you bring them to me?'

Samantha rose, walked around the bed and

tugged open the deep drawer. A smell of mothballs wafted up when she pushed aside some old dress shirts and lifted out a manila envelope and a grey snakeskin box a little smaller than an attaché case. She returned to Alexander and laid them on the bed beside him.

He slid two bound typescripts from the envelope and handed them to her.

She glanced at a cover. *British Museum Monographs. The Development of Ancient Egyptian Funerary Practices. Professor Alexander Meyer. Part One: The Middle Kingdom, Dynasties 11–17.* She gave him a questioning look.

'I tore out the contents, substituted my notes on the drug trafficking. I did it weeks ago, before I was bedridden. All that I know, all that I can remember, is in there. The shipments out of South America, across the Sahara and into Libya and Egypt, the onward distribution into Europe; details of routes, names of people and places, who's paying who. I've marked up some maps — they're in the second binder. You have what Marcus sent you for. You're free to go.'

'I was sent to protect you.'

He gave her a knowing smiled. 'To protect me until you'd found out what I know. And now you can leave.'

'I intend to stay. But I must talk to the nurses and guards, explain my fears, tell them they're under no obligation to remain here. And when Rasha recovers, I'll try to persuade her to leave with Zarina.'

He flicked catches, lifted the lid of the case to reveal a pair of amulets and a necklace arranged in depressions in black velvet. The necklace was heavy and ornate: a cobra and vulture flanking a solar disk and forming a massive pectoral on a chain of tapered gold plates. Alexander gazed at it for a moment, then took a fold of paper from a pocket in the lid. In his thin shaky voice, he read, 'Pectoral of Nufret, high priestess and handmaiden of the god Atum. Gold leaf on bronze, inlaid with lapis lazuli, green felspar and calcite. First dynasty of the New Kingdom. Concealed within the wrappings of a mummy discovered in a side chamber of tomb 32, on the Set Neferu burial site, south of the Valley of Queens at Thebes.' He glanced up at Samantha. 'I'd like you to have this.'

Captivated by the glitter, the brilliance of the colours, but made uneasy by the lavishness of the gift, she hesitated. 'It must be quite valuable.'

'Museums, especially American museums, would pay a great deal for it.' He smiled. I thought you might like to wear it.'

'Surely your wife would love to have it?'

'They frighten her. She won't touch them. Won't even go near them. She thinks they carry curses.' His smile became coaxing. 'Would it repel you to wear a necklace that had adorned a dead priestess?'

'I don't fear the dead, Alexander, only the living. But when would I wear a thing like that? And if it's so valuable, I'd hardly dare to.'

'Wear it for *me*, tonight, after dinner.' His voice lowered, his smile became lascivious. 'Let it cover your naked breasts.'

Samantha laughed. 'We've had this conversation before, Alexander. Slave girls paraded themselves bare-breasted, but priestesses would always be robed.'

'Not when they were making offerings to Atum, enacting the creation ritual, chanting the prayers that — '

'I'm well acquainted with their creation myth, Alexander, you don't have to explain. And if you're suggesting what I think you're suggesting . . . ' she kissed the tip of her index finger and touched it to his lips, ' . . . I'm quite shocked. And what if your wife walked in?' She rose to her feet, picked up the manila envelope and turned towards the door.

'The pectoral, Georgina.' He pushed the case towards her.

'I won't bare my breasts for you, Alexander.'

'I didn't for a moment think you would.' He smiled up at her, then said softly, 'I'd like you to have it, Georgina.'

'Your wife should have it.'

'She loathes the things. Anyway, there are more of them, some solid gold, and many other items that are far more valuable.' His smile became pleading. 'Please, Georgina. It would give a sick old man pleasure.'

Samantha leaned forward, wrapped an arm around his scrawny neck and kissed him, very gently, on the mouth. When he reached up, caressed her cheek and began to respond, she drew away. 'You're incredibly wicked, Alexander; but you're very sweet, and unbelievably generous. I will take the necklace. Thank you.'

'And you'll stay here with me?'

'You didn't have to give me the necklace to persuade me to stay. I'd already decided to remain until you're out of danger.'

'I know,' he said, then his tired voice became wheedling. 'Stay with me until Anubis comes.'

'That could be a very long time, Alexander. I'll stay until you're completely safe, then I'll have to go. And Rasha will soon be well; the last thing she'll want is an intruder in her home.'

'My life, my work, the things stored in the house, they frighten and distress her. You're sympathetic.'

'She's many reasons to be frightened and distressed. Try to be understanding.' Samantha turned and headed for the door. When she was about to step through, he called after her:

'Do you believe in an afterlife, Georgina?'

'Yes. Do you?'

'Throughout my life I've had many intimations of immortality.'

'Does that mean you do?

'I suppose it does.' He frowned thoughtfully. 'Do you think Anubis will come for me?'

'They say God manifests Himself in the mode of the believer.'

'They? Who are *they*?'

'It's something I used to hear my mother say to my father.'

'They were religious people?'

'My mother was a Catholic, very devout; my father was a Jew.'

He gazed at Samantha for a long moment, then said, 'So, you think Anubis might come for me?'

'Quite possibly, Alexander.' She laughed softly. 'When you see the man with the jackal head standing in the doorway, you'll know it's time to go.'

* * *

Samantha leafed through the print-outs of the information the researchers had sent her. Brief details of Dr Suttcliffe, Beckminster Borough Council's director of social services, and Mrs Carver, his head of child protection. Nothing particularly eye-catching. Reginald Suttcliffe's doctorate was in philosophy and he'd been in post for ten years. His wife was called Elaine. They had two children, a boy of fourteen and a girl of sixteen. She was a qualified chiropodist, but no longer practised.

Brenda Carver had been married for fifteen years to a man called Dennis. No children. She'd worked in the Social Services Department for nine years and been promoted to head of child protection four years earlier.

The light had faded and Samantha was finding it difficult to read the documents. She glanced out through the mullioned window. Storm clouds were darkening the sky and the first rumbles of thunder were growling like some great beast beyond the high orchard wall. Rain began to patter against the glass.

She turned back to the desk, clicked on a lamp and ran her eye down the list of landline calls made to and from the Suttcliffes' home. Vet, garage, bank, plumber, and what looked like family and friends: the mundane exchanges of pet-owning people leading quiet, orderly lives. Brenda and Dennis Carver's records were sparse; not many calls were made on their landline. The mobile phone print-outs were more interesting. Samantha cross-checked numbers. Almost every evening, Monday to Friday, Suttcliffe called Carver around 9.30 and the calls were usually of around ten minutes' duration. Saturdays and Sundays, Brenda Carver phoned Suttcliffe at roughly the same time.

Samantha leafed back through the sheets, found the brief notes on Mrs Carver's husband, Dennis. Employed as a technical sales rep by a manufacturer of medical equipment, he covered the North of England, Scotland and Northern Ireland; the sort of job that would take him away from home for most of the week.

Dr Suttcliffe and his wife shared a joint bank account. Samantha studied the entries: Suttcliffe's monthly salary, hefty mortgage payments, the usual household bills, numerous card withdrawals.

Brenda Carver didn't share an account with her husband, but there was nothing unusual on her bank statements: salary in, car-loan repayments out, plenty of card withdrawals, mostly shopping mall things; no household bills, no mortgage payments. Presumably Dennis took care of all that.

The researcher had scribbled a note. *Money transfers from current accounts to what look like deposit accounts, but these not investigated. See large cash transfer (£50,000) to the Suttcliffes' current account from a Jersey-based bank account held by EL Consultancy Services (wife's maiden name is Lawrence). Copies of three recent statements issued by Jersey bank attached.*

Samantha studied the sheets. They'd been sent to an address in Tenby, South Wales, and listed payments, two or three a month, from what appeared to be private-sector care and foster-home providers; round-figure sums, mostly a few hundred pounds, but some as much five thousand. Several large payments had been made by a consortium involved in the provision of secure mental health care: the Rashman-Halim Group.

She relaxed back, pressed the toe of her Ralph Lauren shoe against the leg of the desk and rocked her chair gently to and fro while she took another look through the Suttcliffes' joint-account statements. A few days after the cash injection from the Jersey account they'd made a big payment to a local Audi dealership; probably a car purchase. And there were two monthly standing orders for property tax: one authorizing payments to Beckminster Borough Council; the other to a local authority in Wales.

A terse typewritten note had been included. The sheet was headed: *Re query, Malcombe Bryant, Sergeant, County Police Force. (Son Terry Bryant).* Then continued: *Malcombe Bryant's sister, Vivian Bryant, is listed as a Senior Caseworker on the establishment of Beckminster Borough Council's director of social services. No other connection discovered between Bryant and council and/or teaching staff at school attended by Terry Bryant. Do you want us to dig deeper?*

It was all very interesting. Interesting and useful. Samantha glanced at her watch: almost four. There was still time. She lifted the desk phone, listened to the crackle of lightning on the line as she dialled directory inquiries and asked the operator to connect her to the council offices. A girl with a soft south-country voice answered.

'How may I help you?'

'I'd like to speak to the director of social services.'

'May I ask who's calling?'

'Rachel Travis, Weinman, Wallace and Webster, solicitors, Manchester.'

'Is it miss or missus?'

'Miss.'

'I'll put you through to Dr Suttcliffe's secretary. One moment please.'

The line clicked, distant lightning crackled out of the silence, then it clicked open again. 'Dr Suttcliffe's secretary here, Miss Travis. I'm afraid Dr Suttcliffe's not available. He'll be away from the office until Monday of next week. Perhaps I could find someone else who could help?'

'It's a rather sensitive matter: it concerns a child protection case that's going to court.'

'The only other person who could help is the head of the child protection team, Mrs Carver, but I'm afraid she'll be out of the office until Monday.'

'They're *both* away?' Samantha injected a note of indignation into her voice.

'I'm afraid so, Miss Travis. A senior social worker's conference in Brighton. Dr Suttcliffe's giving the key-note speech. His whole management team is attending. I can't even put you through to a senior caseworker; they're all out, I'm afraid. Is it an urgent matter?

'Very.'

'Would you like me to try to contact Dr Suttcliffe, give him your details and ask him to call you back?'

Samantha concentrated. This wasn't working out. She had to be more inventive. 'I don't think that would be appropriate. It's a dispute Dr Suttcliffe's been helping us with in a private capacity: a contested child protection order. Case is going to trial and we're putting together notes for the barrister. Extracts from a report Dr Suttcliffe prepared are being included. He has to check and initial them. I have to actually meet Dr Sutcliffe. Could you tell me where they're staying in Brighton?'

'Some councillors are included in the party, so the admin people in the Chief Executive's office made a block booking. If you wouldn't mind holding on the line for a moment, I'll put a call through and check. Would that be okay?'

'You're being very kind. Thank you.'

Samantha listened to the rumble of distant thunder; the rain peppering the window.

Presently the line clicked and a voice said, 'Sorry to keep you waiting, Miss Travis. They're all staying at the Majestic, Melville Square. It's on the Kingsway. Would you like me to contact him and let him know you'll be travelling down?'

'Best not,' Samantha cautioned. 'As I said, it concerns advice Dr Suttcliffe's been giving us in a private capacity, not something related to his role as director at Beckminster. It might not please him to know we've discussed it. When I see him, I won't mention our conversation.'

'I'll leave it to you, then, Miss Travis. If there's nothing else?'

'You've already been more than kind.'

Samantha lowered the phone. A drive to Brighton: tonight or first thing tomorrow? Marcus had made it clear that recovering Alexander's wife and children was entirely her concern, added to that, the situation at Sourbeck was worrying, to say the least. It would have to be —

The library door opened and closed; the sound of it almost lost beneath the hiss of pouring rain. Footsteps, faltering and uncertain, approached down the room, then Rasha appeared beyond the opening into the bay window. She'd gathered up her hair, tied it with a black ribbon and applied a smear of lipstick. She paused, her hand resting on the glass top of one of the display cases, and glanced up and down the high, book-lined room. Presently she turned, began to retrace her steps, then caught sight of Samantha behind the desk. 'I . . . I'm so sorry. I didn't mean to intrude.'

Samantha rose and moved towards her. 'You're not intruding, Mrs Meyer, I am. This is your home.' She took her arm. 'Shall we sit down for a moment? I'd like you to tell me how you're feeling.' She steered her towards the leather sofa and settled her into the cushions.

'Feeling?' Rasha managed a weak little

laugh. 'I seem to be incapable of feeling anything. I'm so sleepy — it's as if my head's stuffed with feathers. I can't think. I'm in a constant daze. I . . . ' she shrugged helplessly.

'It's the medicines you've been taking. A day, two days, and you'll be back to normal. Did you know you were heading for the library?'

Rasha's face brightened. 'I suppose I did.'

'Then you're already beginning to remember things again.'

'I . . . I was looking for Amir and Maria.'

'They're not here,' Samantha said softly. She reached for Rasha's hand.

'Not here?'

'They were taken into care, by the local authority.'

'Taken into care?' Rasha looked at her, bewildered.

'It's rather complicated. It started when you went to the children's school. Someone had made a complaint about Zarina. Do you remember?'

'I thought that was a dream. I have so many dreams. Dreams of struggling and fighting, being driven away in a car, locked in a police cell. And . . . and being in the dark and feeling cool air on my skin, and hands touching me — intimately — and a fragrance, tangy, bitter-sweet, rather like oranges.'

Samantha drew a deep breath and tried to hold back a rush of anger. Rasha had already suffered so much; there was no point dwelling on this, no point causing her even more distress. Keeping her voice calm, she said, 'It must have been the drugs they were giving you in the hospital. Memories and dreams: they become confused, one with the other. But you did struggle with a social worker, and the police did take you away.'

'But I've never hit anyone in my life. I — '

'Tomorrow, Rasha. When you're feeling better. I'll explain it all then.'

'And Amir and Maria, where — '

'They're being cared for.'

'Cared for? Who is caring for them?'

'The authorities; the council's social services department. Try not to worry. I'm going to bring them back to you.'

Rasha closed her eyes; abandoned herself to confusion and helplessness. Her lips had parted, they were trembling, and her mouth was making an ugly shape. 'God, I feel so tired,' she whimpered. 'Too tired to think. Too tired to even care about my babies . . . ' Samantha squeezed her hand. She had to get the children back before the sedation wore off. 'And Alex looks so old and thin and grey. I don't recognize him any more. I . . . I find him quite repulsive.' She opened her eyes.

'Have I shocked you?'

Samantha shook her head.

'But I did love him: in a gentle, contented way, you understand. And he was so good to me, and so kind to Zarina. Sometimes it made me jealous: I felt ashamed of being jealous of my own daughter. She's not his child, did you know that? But he's been as kind to her as he is to his own children. Perhaps it was because she was older, because he could talk to her about the things that interested him.' Rasha's voice trailed away. She seemed to be trying to order her thoughts. Presently she sighed, and said, 'Zarina's father was my great love, the love that overwhelmed and consumed me, my grand passion.' She glanced at Samantha. 'Are you married?'

'I'm a widow.'

'Do you understand what I mean when I say my great love, my grand passion?'

'Perfectly. It's an experience we've shared.'

'I would have done anything for him, gone anywhere with him, but when I told him I was pregnant he wanted nothing more to do with me. Afterwards, I saw him once or twice, sweeping past in his big black limousine. Sometimes he saw me, but he just looked away; he never acknowledged me. He was a diplomat, tall and handsome, very distinguished.' She sniffed back tears. 'Alexander was a far more decent man. He truly loved me. And he's been so kind to me, and so proud of me, and I did love him, but not in the way I loved Zarina's father. That can happen only once in a woman's life. If she's very lucky, it will be the man she marries. If she is not so lucky, it will be an affair.' She sighed. 'Alexander has given me so much, and I've given him so little.'

Her gaze began to wander over the book-lined walls. The storm had darkened the room. Here and there a gilded binding gleamed when the lightning flickered. Thunder growled. The storm seemed to be coming nearer, and the atmosphere had become heavy and oppressive. Rasha searched Samantha's face with frightened eyes. 'He's dying, isn't he?'

Samantha nodded.

'Will it be soon?'

Samantha shrugged. 'A week, two weeks, perhaps a month.'

'Then I must try very hard to overcome my revulsion.'

* * *

'You're not wearing a dress tonight.' Zarina was sitting on the edge of Samantha's bed, looking with interest at her black roll-neck sweater and black jeans, her black lace-up boots with thick rubber soles.

'I'm low on dresses. I've managed to have a couple cleaned in Beckminster, but I need to go home to Crispin.'

'Do you miss him?'

'Yes.'

'Do you think he misses you?'

Samantha laughed. 'You ask the most searching questions. A little, possibly. He's very taken up with his own affairs.'

'What are you reading?'

'Notes on some people. I'm trying to memorize the details. I hope to meet them tomorrow.'

'They're coming here?'

'I'm going to see them in Brighton.'

'Alexander took us all to Brighton last year. We had lunch in a big hotel. Maria was sick and Mummy got angry, but Alexander said funny things to make her laugh and she was okay again. We had a lovely time.'

'Where is your mother?'

'In her bedroom. She has pictures of us all on her dressing table, arranged around statues of the Virgin and St Anthony. She lights candles and says prayers. Bit like casting spells, except spells work better.'

Samantha looked up from her papers. Thunder was still rumbling but the rain had stopped. It had become cooler, almost chilly. She smiled. 'Don't confuse occult mumbo-jumbo with seeking the intercession of the saints.'

'Spells work,' Zarina insisted. 'The storm came and flooded the house; that nasty woman had to go back into hospital.'

'Sheer coincidence.'

Zarina relaxed back on the bed and propped herself on her elbows. 'I've copied more spells from the grimoire: spells for healing the sick and finding lost treasure. I suppose Maria and Amir could be called lost treasures. And today I gathered all the things I'll need.'

'The things you'll need?'

'Some of Alexander's hair, a pair of Maria's knickers and one of Amir's old shoes.'

'And how did you get Alexander's hair?'

'Waited until the nurse took the plastic sacks down to the back yard, then went in with the scissors. He was sort of drowsy. He just smiled at me, and I cut some hair off. I'll go down to the quarry tomorrow, sweep the altar and do the invocations.'

'Not tomorrow,' Samantha said. 'And not until I say you can.'

Zarina sat up on the bed, her face petulant. 'But I must. I want Alexander to get better; I want Maria and Amir to — '

'It's dangerous. The grounds are too big for the men to patrol, and heaven knows who's wandering around out there. You must stay in the house and the rear yard.'

'Nathan will take me.'

'I've told Nathan to stay close to the house. It's too dangerous even for him.' Samantha made her voice stern. 'Do the spells in the attic if you must, but don't leave the house.'

'I need the altar and the pentagram.'

'Say prayers with your mother. Leave occult things alone. I want you to promise me — '

The radio-phone began to bleep. Samantha snatched it from the bedside table and keyed it on.

'There's an intruder, ma'am.'

'Where?'

'Climbing over the back gate.'

'Where are you?'

'On the roof, patrolling behind the parapets.'

'Come down to the bedroom corridor and keep watch outside Professor Meyer's room.'

'He's sitting astride the gate now, ma'am, helping someone up . . . There's two of them, wearing waterproof anoraks with the hoods up . . . They're dropping into the rear yard.'

'Don't let them know they've been seen.

I'll go down to the kitchen and watch from there. Then I'll deal with it.'

'You want me to come with you, ma'am?'

'Where's Jack?'

'By the main gates.'

'Stay close to the bedrooms.' Samantha dragged her gun, still in its holster, from the bed, swung it around her shoulders and buckled the strap. She fixed Zarina in a meaningful stare. 'See what I mean? It's dangerous. Don't you dare go out of the house. Stay with your mother.'

The rear yard was hidden from her. Nathan had done his rounds of the ground-floor rooms, closed the wooden shutters and dropped the iron bars that locked them in place. Even if she were careful, exposing the kitchen window would make quite a clatter. She unlocked the back door, opened it a little and peered out. A thick blanket of cloud obscured the night sky. The cobbled yard, the old horse trough, the outbuildings and stables, were featureless shapes, shrouded in darkness. She heard whispering and tried to locate the sound. Presently she saw them, shadowy forms, lurking by the open front of the stable block, close to the Peugeot driven by the Americans. They turned and looked towards the house, their hooded faces pale smudges in the gloom, then disappeared into the stable.

Samantha slid her gun from its holster, stepped out of the kitchen and skirted puddles as she made her way across the yard. She could see them now. One was tugging at the car doors; the other was trying to lever open the rear hatch. Words whispered in Spanish were being garnished with American expletives. She took a firm grip on the gun. 'Step away from the car, put your hands behind — '

The man near the hatch leaned back and hurled something. Samantha stepped sideways and squeezed the trigger. In the fading echoes of the crash she heard metal clattering on stone and glanced down. A gardener's fork, probably the thing he'd been using to prize open the hatch, was lying on the cobbles.

'Out,' Samantha snapped at the one still standing. 'Come out into the yard where I can see you.'

Ignoring her, he scrambled round the car, wailing, 'Ricardo, Ricardo.'

'You're wasting your time. He's dead. Come out into the yard or I'll kill you.'

'Bitch,' he whimpered. 'You murdering bitch. You shot my brother, you've — '

'Pull your hood down, get your hands behind your head, and come out here. I'm going to count to three: one . . . '

He emerged into the yard.

'Not too close.' Samantha menaced him with the gun.

'My brother needs help. You've got to get him some help. A doctor, an ambulance.'

'He's dead. How many more times do I have to say it? And you will be too if you don't stop whining. Now, move over to that door.' He began to shuffle off. 'Not the house door, the laundry door, the one near the water butt.'

He changed direction.

'Open it wide and switch on the light. The switch is just inside the opening.'

The door thudded against the wall. He fumbled for the switch. When the light came on, Samantha saw he was young; twenty-five, thirty; straight black hair, broad shoulders, medium height. His sloe-black eyes were round and bright with fear, his chin was trembling.

'Lie down on the floor, face down.'

'My brother needs help,' he wailed. 'Get someone to — '

'He's dead. Lie down on the floor, face down, head towards me.'

He fell to his knees, then prostrated himself, his face resting on his arms. She knelt beside him, stabbed the muzzle of the gun in the small of his back, then deftly hooked a handcuff around one of his ankles. After she'd squeezed the ratchet tight, she clipped the other cuff around the iron support of a massive porcelain sink, then rose and stepped back.

He pushed himself into a sitting position.

'Your name,' Samantha demanded. 'Tell me your name?'

'Bitch! Get an ambulance for my — '

She swung the gun, slicing it down the side of his head. He moaned. Blood began to ooze from a jagged gash.

'Your brother's dead, and you're going to tell me everything I want to know. We'll start with your name, then you can tell me why you were so interested in a car you couldn't possibly get out of a locked yard.'

12

The Majestic Hotel was imposing. Victoriana at its very best. Wedding-cake white, its ornate facade faced towards the sea and its many windows were reflecting the sparkling marine light.

Samantha had parked beside gardens that filled the centre of the square. She was waiting for the cleaners to get into their mid-morning routine before venturing inside; trying to decide whether or not to give Marcus a progress report. She decided she would, found the encrypted mobile amongst the clutter in her bag and keyed in the number.

The faint bleeping stopped and a refined voice, made curt by irritation, said, 'That you, Sam? I've been trying to reach you for ages. Have you got anything out of Alexander?'

'Not yet, Marcus, but I'm getting close. Tomorrow, day after, I should be able to start feeding material through.' He hadn't asked how she was, how the professor was. The information was the only thing he cared about.

'Chief's getting very restless, and the

Americans are angry. They've started complaining through political channels; they're accusing us of floundering around.'

'The Americans are convinced we always flounder around.' She changed the subject. 'Caught two intruders last night. Killed one, interrogated the other. Brothers: Ricardo and Pepe Lujan, sons of Renato Lujan.'

'The Lujan family — one of the Colombian big three.'

'Probably one of the Colombian big two now. The American agents I caught prowling around the place, the FBI man and the CIA man, were fed information by the Lujans so they could close down competitors. In return, the Lujans were left alone to develop the drug trade through Africa into Europe. Seems the agents were given other perks, too. They'd driven to the UK through Spain and France and the car they were using was loaded with fifty kilos of cocaine: false floor, false bulkheads. Their ID cards would have got them through border posts and customs.'

'You've got the car?'

'It's in the stables at the back of the house. The brothers had come looking for it. The Lujans are convinced the agents managed to contact Alexander. Now they're afraid they've been infiltrated; that the enforcement agencies are going to move in and shut down the traffic to and across Africa.'

A middle-aged woman, thin legs exposed by a short beach dress, trotted past the car, arm in arm with a grey-haired man in a blazer and jaunty yachting cap.

She went on: 'Pepe said they were shipping out a million dollars worth of cocaine a day before the regime change disrupted things. Old Renato's concerned because so many people are getting a cut: Al-Qaida, tribal leaders, officials, government ministers. There's too much cash trickling down. They know who the big players are, but they don't have a very clear picture about the rest. They want to get in amongst it and eliminate the hangers on. If necessary, make changes to the supply routes and establish a fresh network. Renato's desperate to discover what Alexander knows.

'That's all I could get out of Pepe last night. He was in a pretty bad way at the end. I'll try again when he's recovered a little. He kept making veiled threats about retribution. There's something happening. I think they're planning an assault on the Hall.'

'Have you talked to Alexander about him moving out?'

'I have and he won't. I told him the guards and the nurses shouldn't be exposed to the danger. He said let them go. He knows he's dying, he knows it's going to be soon, and he's determined to die where he was born.'

'I presume his wife and children are still missing?'

'Wife's back. I rescued her from a private psychiatric hospital run by an Iraqi refugee masquerading as a doctor: a man called Nuwaf Al-Museck. He's wanted by the Iraqi authorities for murder and sexually assaulting female patients. I'm pretty sure he raped Rasha Meyer on a nightly basis, but she was too heavily sedated to realize what was happening.'

'Dear God,' Marcus breathed. For once he sounded shocked.

'Do you want his details so you can pass them on to the Iraqis or the immigration people?'

'Immigration are under a lot of pressure. Iraq's in chaos after we trashed it, and they aren't accepting the return of refugees. If Immigration arrest him they might not be able to deport him. No one's going to be interested, Sam. Just forget it and concentrate on finding out what Alexander knows.'

Samantha closed her eyes and tried to control her anger.

'Sam . . . ? You still there, Sam?'

'I'm still here, Marcus.'

'Where are you now?'

'In the library, at the Hall, waiting for

Alexander to come round.' She smiled, taking a malicious pleasure in the duplicity, then embroidered the fabrication. 'He usually has a few lucid hours in the middle of the day.'

'You'll contact me immediately you have something?'

'Of course.'

'Just concentrate on that, Sam. Forget everything else. Nothing else matters but that.'

She clicked off the phone.

Marcus was a callous bastard. Even so, it was strange he hadn't been more concerned about Alexander refusing to move out. The nurses, the doctor, the guards, had been sent in to prolong his life and keep him safe. Either Marcus didn't share her fears about an assault being made on the Hall, or his patience was running out and he no longer cared. Perhaps Loretta had been giving him so much grief about the delay and the cost he was abandoning the exercise. It wouldn't be difficult to have something cobbled together to appease the Americans; tell them the report was a bit threadbare because Alexander hadn't known as much as he'd claimed. They'd certainly swallow that.

She gazed across the sunlit gardens while she took stock of the situation. One of the nurses had agreed to stay, one had already quit and the other was leaving when her shift ended that afternoon. One of the guards was taking leave, but they hadn't arranged a replacement. Another had already worked too many hours without rest days. That would mean, for a while at least, that there was only one she could call on to watch the gate and the house. Patrolling the grounds would be completely out of the question.

If the Lujans came, they'd probably come in the night. Pepe Lujan had said: 'It won't be long. Men are being hired, strong men, men who are armed and men who can handle dogs. When my father arrives, he will organize them. Then they will come for you, and you will pay for what you have done to my brother and me.'

Dogs? Were they thinking of bringing dogs? And he'd hinted at quite a large gang of men. Perhaps they were convinced the house and grounds were well guarded: everyone who'd tried to enter the place had disappeared. And perhaps they anticipated some skirmishes amongst the trees. Vicious fighting dogs would be a formidable and expendable asset in a situation like that, especially in the dark.

When would they come? The search for Amir and Maria was going to keep her away from the Hall tonight. Should she abandon it and go back? That could cause problems.

Rasha was only coping with the situation because of the lingering effects of the drugs, and they were wearing off. Tomorrow she might be beside herself, frantic with worry, unable cope with what had been done to her.

Samantha dropped the phone in her bag. She'd come this far, she may as well try to recover Amir and Maria. If, by dawn tomorrow, she'd got nowhere, she'd abandon the attempt and return to the Hall. She slipped on sunglasses, gathered up her bag and climbed out of the Ferrari. She smoothed the skirt of her blue and backless Bottega Veneta dress — the dry cleaners in Beckminster had done a very respectable job — then, high heels tapping, she headed up the rise to the Majestic.

* * *

The lift lurched to a stop, its doors rumbled open and Samantha stepped out on to the third floor. The place had been completely refurbished: carpets were deep and new, the rather grand public rooms had been tastefully decorated, the bedrooms modernized.

A housekeeper's trolley was parked along the corridor and discarded sheets and pillowcases were spilling out of a wheeled bin. A vacuum cleaner was droning in one of the bedrooms. Samantha headed towards the sound and discovered a tall girl in brown overalls manoeuvring the machine around the bed.

Senses dulled by the noise, she was oblivious to everything except her job.

Samantha touched her arm. She turned, startled, then switched off the machine. 'Madam?'

Samantha smiled. 'You're from Poland?' Close up, what she'd taken to be a girl was clearly a woman of more than thirty, brown-eyed, with a summer tan and mousy hair swept behind her ears. Her answering smile was friendly. She seemed approachable; someone who'd be interested in earning a little extra money, someone who'd be willing.

The woman looked surprised. 'You speak my language?'

'Quite well. May we talk?'

'I'm so busy. We are kept on a tight schedule. Fifteen rooms each, and today I do more because one of the girls is sick.'

'I won't keep you long, and I think what I have to say is going to interest you.' Samantha returned to the door and closed it, then opened her ID wallet and exposed her personal card: *Georgina Grey Investigations*. 'Shall we sit on the bed?'

The woman joined her. She was giving

Samantha wary, nervous looks.

'My client's husband is staying at the hotel,' Samantha explained. 'She thinks he's having an affair with a colleague. He denies it, but she doesn't believe him. She's asked me to get evidence.'

'So?'

'I need a master pass card to operate the door locks. I have to get inside their room and take pictures. Would you let me borrow your card when you finish work? I'd bring it back to you early in the morning.' She clicked open her bag and took out an envelope.

'I couldn't. The cards are given out by the housekeeper. They have to be handed in at the end of each shift.'

Samantha began to count out slim bundles of bank notes. 'Are they always handed in?'

'Sometimes girls leave for home and forget, but there's always trouble. One or two have been dismissed for it. It's taken very seriously.'

Samantha fanned out the bundles of notes. 'Five hundred pounds for the use of the pass card, another two hundred if you can tell me the room numbers of the people I'm interested in.' I'll hand over the cash when you lend me the card.'

'Seven hundred pounds?'

Samantha nodded.

The woman chewed her lip. It was so tempting. And she could tell Mrs Langdon she'd stay on and do more rooms. Sometimes, when she did that, Mrs Langdon left before she'd finished, and not signing the card back in wouldn't be such a problem. She took a deep breath. 'Okay, I'll do it. But I must have the card back before seven in the morning. If you don't get it back to me I'll — '

'I'll get it back to you long before that.'

'I don't care what time you wake me up, just get the card back to me.'

Samantha returned the money to her bag. 'Where shall we meet, and what time?'

'The back of the hotel runs right through to Bridewell Street. Meet me there. I'll tell them I'll do some more rooms, so about four o'clock. That okay?'

'That's fine. Look for a red Ferrari; there's not likely to be more than one. I'll drive you home.'

'It's quite a way out of town.'

'Don't worry. I need to know where you live so I can return the card.'

* * *

Dr Suttcliffe's keynote speech was a rather lengthy disquisition he'd entitled *Conflicts of Freedom and Restraint in the Care of*

Vulnerable Adolescents. While he was delivering it, Samantha made a tour of some stands advertising healthcare services. A rep for a consortium of foster home providers told her they were organizing a dinner for the delegates. It was to be held that night, and Dr Suttcliffe was guest of honour. The rep invited her to come as his guest. He was charmingly persuasive. She was equally charming when she declined.

One of the staff setting out the dining room for the venue told her they expected the proceedings to wind up no later than ten, as the delegates would be impatient to avail themselves of a free bar laid on by a manufacturer of mobility aids. The information had put a timetable on things.

The Polish woman who cleaned rooms was called Anna. When she handed over the pass card she told Samantha that Dr Suttcliffe had a rather splendid double room on the second floor; Mrs Carver a more modest single on the fourth. If they were indulging in an extramarital affair, there was little doubt where they'd conduct their trysts.

Anna was bright. She seemed to know instinctively what would be helpful. She described the layout of Dr Suttcliffe's room in some detail. On the lobby side of the bathroom wall, near the entrance door, was a duct that hid the cables and waste pipes that ran from floor to floor. The flushing cistern for the toilet in the bathroom was fixed in there, too. Sometimes maintenance men had to repair leaks or fix the cisterns, and the enclosed space had to be cleaned afterwards. The duct door was opened with a special key, and every housekeeping trolley carried one. Samantha was slender. She would be able to squeeze up against the pipes, so Anna had brought the key for the duct as well as the pass card for the doors. Samantha gave her an extra hundred pounds.

It was a little after 9.30. Soon the dinner for the delegates would be winding up. Samantha swept the master card past the lock, heard it click, then pushed open the door and entered Dr Suttcliffe's room. An earlier search of Brenda Carver's room had revealed nothing of interest: just a few fairly ordinary summer clothes and some items of expensive underwear. She switched on the lights. The duct Anna had described was hidden in a shadowy corner behind the entrance door. When she swung open the access panel she saw pipes and electrical cables; a flushing cistern was bolted to the back wall. If she rested her posterior on the rim of the cistern, she'd be able to squeeze inside. She checked the surprisingly large bathroom, then moved into the bedroom area.

A laptop, conference papers, and a copy of Dr Suttcliffe's speech, double-space typed and covered in cryptic notes, were neatly arranged on a small writing desk. Brenda Carver's nightdress, some tights and a few pairs of knickers were secreted away in a drawer; Reginald Suttcliffe's blue-striped cotton pyjamas were neatly folded on one of the pillows. A suit and a couple of shirts were on hangers in the wardrobe; the rest of his clothes were still in a suitcase.

Time to conceal herself. She switched off the lights and stepped into the duct. The iron pipes felt rough and cold against her naked back, the top of the flushing cistern cut into her thigh, but she managed to squeeze inside. She gripped the inner framework of the access panel, swung it almost shut and settled down to wait.

She didn't have to wait long before she heard the lock on the outer door click and feet padding over carpet. Samantha drew the duct cover completely shut. A body fell against it, and a woman's laughter was suddenly interrupted by kissing sounds and heavy breathing. There was some fumbling against the panel, then a man's voice said, 'God, I just had to do that.'

A woman laughed, then whispered, 'I'm glad you did.'

After more kissing, the man said, 'It's the dress.' His deep, refined voice was breathless. 'That new graduate trainee couldn't take his eyes off you. What's his name? Darren, Derek something or other?'

'David Bicknell.' Her voice became teasing. 'I think he's quite handsome in that boyish kind of way, and he's very polite and respectful. Not like the usual intake.'

'He couldn't keep his greedy little eyes off your tits.' More kissing sounds.

The woman laughed and gasped for breath. 'Were you jealous?'

'Madly. Your tits belong to me.'

She laughed again. 'I like it when you're jealous. Shall we turn in?'

'Isn't that why we came up?'

The bodies pushed themselves off the duct panel. Seconds later, a woman's voice, fainter now, said, 'Come and unzip me.'

'Do you think they suspect?' the man asked.

'I'm pretty sure they don't. I told Pauline I had a migraine; said I was going up to take some aspirin and have an early night. I left the *Do Not Disturb* sign on the door. Anyway, everyone's gone to that free bar the mobility aids people have laid on. Can't remember the firm's name, but I've got their literature.'

Shoes scraped on tiles, the toilet seat clattered against the partition and someone Samantha took to be a man relieved himself rather noisily. Levers clanked, water gushed, then the cistern began to fill again.

There was breathless laughter, faint, from the bedroom, and a woman's voice begged, 'Not yet, Reggie. I want to brush my teeth and I need the toilet. I won't be comfortable.'

'But Brenda, *I need you.* We're talking sheer bloody desperation here.'

More girlish laughter, then, 'I'll only be two minutes. Surely you can wait that long? Just fold the covers back and get into bed.'

The toilet seat dropped. Seconds later, levers clanked and the cistern flushed again. Fainter sounds of running water followed, then the bathroom door opened and feet padded away across the carpet.

'I was so proud of you today, Reggie.' Brenda Carver's voice was just audible. 'No one but you could have written such a perfect speech; no one could have delivered it better. You were so . . . Reggie, darling!'

Shocked laughter, then a deep voice was murmuring indistinct words that turned into grunts interspersed with faint little cries.

Things were taking their primordial course. Samantha eased the duct door open and emerged into the tiny lobby. The sounds were clearer now. His breathing had become harsh and ragged; her little cries more urgent. A glow through the opening told her they'd left the bedside lamps on. She took a tiny camera from her bag, set it for continuous shots, then moved on into the bedroom.

Soft light from a pair of pink-shaded lamps gleamed on Reggie's bald patch, cast a glow over his broad back and lardy buttocks, intensified the darkness of the hair that smothered his arms and legs. Brenda's plump and rather shapely calves were folded over the small of his back, her ankles were crossed; the nails of her delicate little toes had been painted a soft pink. A hint of cellulite rippled over her thighs. Her eyes were tightly closed; her lips parted.

Samantha pressed the shutter. The camera began to flash. At first, the lovers were too engrossed in one another to notice the flickering light, then Reggie's buttocks stopped heaving and his head turned. Brenda's lashes fluttered. When her eyes opened she let out a little scream. Samantha moved in to get a close-up.

'Who the hell are you?' Reggie rolled onto his back. Shock spawned a sudden anger and he was almost shouting when he repeated, 'Who the hell are you, and what the devil do you think you're doing?'

Samantha slid the gun from her bag. With

the silencer fitted it was even more intimidating. 'Just recording your happy moments, Reggie.'

'I said, who are you?' His voice had lowered to an angry snarl.

She dropped the camera into her bag, took out her ID wallet and displayed the Serious Crime card.

'What do you want with us?' His tone was wary now. Suddenly aware of his nakedness, he cupped his hands over his genitals.

Brenda was squeezing her legs together; concealing her breasts with her arms and hands. Her shocked, wide-eyed look darkened into a scowl. 'I know you,' she said indignantly. 'You visited my office, talked about a woman who'd been sectioned and had her children taken into care.'

Samantha plucked Nuwaf Al-Museck's letter from her bag, unfolded it and handed it to Suttcliffe. 'Mrs Meyer's no longer in psychiatric care. The doctor's released her. She's at home. If you read to the end you'll see he's recommending the immediate return of her children. That's why I'm here. I want Rasha Meyer's children.'

Suttcliffe passed the letter to Brenda Carver then whipped his hand back to his genitals.

'I want them to be given to me no later than noon tomorrow.'

'That's quite out of question. Even if Dr Asadi recommends their return, we still have to make our own assessment. And if we agree they should be returned, there are procedures to be followed.'

'Forget assessments, forget procedures. Noon tomorrow or your wife and her husband get the photos.'

'That's blackmail, and I will not be intimidated.' He reached for the bedside phone.

Samantha pressed the muzzle of the silencer against his throat. 'You don't realize what deep shit you and your lady friend have waded into, Reggie. I'm a woman in a hurry; I'm prepared to take any measures. Bit like your organization, really, only I don't have to rely on court hearings behind closed doors, undisclosed evidence, secret reports, dodgy expert witnesses. I just get on with the job.'

'What utter rubbish. Everything we do is in the interests of the child. And we obey the law; follow procedures that ensure — '

'Shall we talk about the statements from your bank in Jersey, the ones listing payments from foster and care home providers? Putting the consultancy firm in your wife's maiden name won't do, Reggie. She was a chiropodist, not a child care expert. The only things she could advise on are corns and in-growing toenails. You've been taking back-handers on a heroic scale. A placement must be worth thousands to a care provider. They'd be grateful for every child and vulnerable adult you could send.'

Brenda Carver was staring at him. 'You've never said anything about that to me, Reggie.'

'It's lies,' he snarled. 'She's bluffing. I do a little private consultancy work; everyone knows about it, the council have sanctioned it. What she's saying is absolutely preposterous.'

Samantha took the bank statements from her bag and tossed them over to Brenda. 'Take a look. If all of those payments are for private consultancy work he's never had time to do a thing for Beckminster Borough Council.'

Brenda's gaze slid down the columns of figures. Reginald closed his eyes. Big hands still cupping his genitals, he let his head fall back on the pillows.

'The children,' Samantha repeated. 'Amir and Maria: I want them handed over to me tomorrow.'

'I'm not going to allow you to bully us into precipitate — '

Samantha made her voice threatening. 'No more talk. You've got the letter recommending the return to the mother. I get the children tomorrow. Any slip-ups and your partners get the photos and the district auditor gets the bank statements.'

He jerked his head up from the pillows. 'This is outrageous. Documents have to be prepared, forms completed, and they all require *my* signature.'

Samantha pointed the gun at Brenda Carver. 'She can prepare the documents and sign them per-pro.' She smiled at her. 'Time to get out of bed and put your knickers on, Brenda. We're going to Beckminster. I'm sure one of you will have keys to the offices. You can put the paperwork together tonight and have the children collected and brought to me after breakfast tomorrow.'

The lovers seemed numb now; too shocked to speak. Samantha smiled down at them. 'You want me to send the pictures to Dennis and Elaine, the Jersey bank statements to the auditor?'

Brenda slid from the bed, found her knickers beneath the rumpled sheet and pulled them on. 'How are we going to do the actual transfer? After what happened to Catherine I won't be able to persuade anyone to visit the house without a police escort.'

'There's a cafe in Beckminster called the Pink Banana; they specialize in ice creams. I'll be waiting there at eleven with their sister, Zarina.'

Brenda paused in her dressing. 'We were told Zarina had gone back to Egypt.'

'And if you'd done a more thorough investigation, if you'd found the child and interviewed her, you'd have known she was never abused in her present home. The abuse occurred years ago, when she lived with her mother's family in Egypt. And the mother took her away as soon as she found out. You'd absolutely no grounds for taking her brother and sister into care and causing so much unspeakable suffering.'

'Don't listen to this, Brenda. The woman doesn't know what she's talking about. Ignore her.'

'Ignore her? Get real, Reggie. I don't want Dennis to find out about us. And what about Elaine and the children? What would it do to them? And I was never happy about the Meyer case. Vivian Bryant just wouldn't let it go. She organized that first inspection. If it hadn't been for her the Meyer woman would never have been sectioned.'

'We'd had reports. She was just following procedures.'

'She went over my head to you, and you listened, and when the mother was sectioned it was you who approved her being placed in that psychiatric hospital, even though we'd had warnings.'

He nodded meaningfully towards Samantha and hissed, 'I think you've said enough.'

'Said enough? She probably knows far more about you and the Department than I do, Reggie. Didn't you read her ID card? I'm going back to Beckminster. I'll do the paperwork tonight. Lucy handled the actual foster home placement. First thing tomorrow, I'll take her with me when I collect the children.' She turned to Samantha. 'What about the things in my room?'

'Why not leave them? Travel back tomorrow. Carry on as if nothing had happened.' She smiled. 'We can all keep secrets.'

13

Five-year-old Amir, and Maria, who was six, had been told that their mother and father had died, that their sister had gone back to Egypt, that they'd be found new mummies and daddies soon, but they might not be able to stay together.

Home again, they were silent and withdrawn, possessed by a nervousness that escalated into terror whenever their mother left the room. The change in them distressed Zarina. It induced in their mother a cold and bitter anger. Rasha was able to think and feel again.

They were sitting in the big salon at the front of the house. Late-afternoon sun, slanting through tall windows, was making dust motes glitter and filling the shabby room with a soft golden light. Amir and Maria were clinging to their mother on the huge slab-sided sofa. Samantha was sitting in a high-backed chair beside the ornate fireplace.

Rasha poured coffee into tiny cups. Zarina carried one over to Samantha. 'You say my children were in a foster home?'

Samantha nodded, added sugar, then said,

'A privately run place on the outskirts of Beckminster, I gather.'

'Why would anyone want to do such a thing to us?'

'You visited Zarina's school, humiliated a police sergeant in front of his wife and son; made the teachers look like fools. The police sergeant's sister is one of the council's child welfare officers. She helped them to take their revenge.'

'Can petty officials behave like that in England? In Egypt one expects malice, but here — '

'The headmistress questioned Zarina and learned about her great-uncle. She presumed the things she described were happening here and now. She passed the information on to the child welfare people and it gave them grounds to act.'

Rasha's mouth hardened with anger. She folded the children in her arms, Maria began to suck her thumb, and three pairs of bewildered brown eyes searched Samantha's face, looking for some assurance that everything was going to be all right, that no one would come to their home and traumatize them in this way again.

Samantha said, 'I have to talk with you, on your own.'

'After dinner, perhaps, when the children

are sleeping? The housekeeper's abandoned us and I'm trying to prepare one of Alexander's favourite meals.'

'When we've finished this coffee,' Samantha insisted. 'Your bedroom would be the best place. While we're talking, the children can look in on Alexander.'

* * *

Samantha stood in the hall, listening to the silence of the house. After taking food to the Colombian imprisoned in the laundry, she'd snatched a couple of hours' sleep while Rasha attended to the children. Their talk hadn't been completely fruitless. Rasha had refused to leave that night, but she'd agreed to Samantha making arrangements for her and the children to move out the next day. Her head had cleared. Receptive now to Samantha's warnings, she understood that they were in danger.

The heavy entrance door had been bolted, the ground-floor windows shuttered, the iron bars dropped in place. But these things merely gave an illusion of security; determined men could easily force their way in. The guards hadn't seen any intruders whilst she'd been away in Brighton. Today there had only been one guard, but he'd had nothing to report. Rasha and the children had retired for the night. The nurse who'd agreed to stay was watching over Alexander. Nathan had discarded his huge boots and was snoozing in an old rocking chair in the kitchen. The big house was quiet and still.

Samantha settled her gun holster more comfortably around her shoulders, then climbed the stairs to her room. She crossed over to the window and drew the curtains aside. An almost full moon was bathing the forecourt and the enclosing trees in its silvery spectral light, leaching out colours, darkening shadows.

A bleeping sounded. Samantha snatched up the radio-phone from her bedside table. 'Charlie . . . Charlie . . . ?' There was no answering voice, just a faint background hiss, a crackle of static.

She heard the drone of engines. The sound was coming closer. Stepping back to the window, she looked towards the driveway and watched the headlights of approaching cars grow brighter, then become dazzling, as they drew near. Two four-by-fours, a large saloon, two black vans and another four-by-four rumbled on to the forecourt. A man jumped from the lead car and began waving his arms, directing the others to park close to the trees, facing the house.

There were rough voices, van doors slamming, dogs barking, men cursing in some East European tongue. A grey-haired man, broad-shouldered and stocky, climbed out of the big saloon. Reaching through a sidelight, he made the horn blare, then yelled, 'I want you, Meyer!' His hoarse voice was forceful and demanding, his accent Spanish. He made the horn blare again: three long blasts. 'I am Renato Lujan. I have come to talk with you. Come on out, Meyer. We have your daughter.' He turned and gestured. The man who'd directed the parking reached into a four-by-four, lifted Zarina out and stood her on the bonnet. 'It's the child called Zarina: your little witch, your *bruja*. One of my men found her earlier, dancing around a fire, chanting like a shaman. Come for her, Meyer. Just you. Leave your men inside, so we can talk.'

Anger and fear surged through Samantha. The stupid child, disobeying her like that. She reached under the old brass bed and dragged out the Heckler sub machine gun and box of grenades. When she turned to leave the room, she saw Rasha standing in the doorway.

'What is all that shouting and barking and horns blowing?'

'A gang of men. They've come for your husband. They don't know that he's ill.'

Rasha moved past her and peered through the window. 'There are so many.'

'They probably believe we have many men in here.'

'And all those crazy dogs. Why bring dogs?'

'They're fighting dogs. Very useful if things get out of hand.'

Rasha suddenly gasped and clutched at her throat. 'They've got Zarina.' She turned and stared at Samantha with wide and terrified eyes. 'I thought she was in her room. Do something. For God's sake, do something.'

Do something? Do what? More than a dozen men and a pack of dogs, and Zarina on display making it impossible to use the Heckler or hurl grenades down from the roof. She took Rasha's arm and pulled her away from the window. 'Where are the children sleeping?'

'With me. They won't let me out of their sight.'

'Take them into a room at the back, settle them down on the floor and try to secure the door.'

'What about Alexander?'

'The nurse is with him. He's had his morphine. He'll be out of it.' She gave Rasha a push. 'Move the children to the back. Do it now.'

Samantha drew the strap of the Heckler

over her shoulder, picked up the box of grenades, then ran down to the kitchen. She roused Nathan, looked into his startled face and mouthed, 'Man in the laundry,' she handed him the key to the handcuffs, 'unfasten him and bring him into the hall. Okay?'

He nodded and reached for his boots.

Samantha raced back along the passage to the hall, laid the box of grenades on a small, semi-circular table, then slid her encrypted mobile from a pouch on her belt and pressed keys. The 'no-signal' icon winked back at her. She snatched up the house phone and dialed. Silence. Nothing. Not even a hiss. The line through the trees had been cut. Three women, three children, a dying man and a deaf mute, were at the mercy of an armed gang and a pack of crazy fighting dogs.

She lifted the lid of the box and gazed down at the cluster of khaki-coloured spheres. About the size of a tennis ball, fitted with a metal cap and detonating lever, some were marked with a red band, some with a yellow. She glanced at the leaflet pasted on the underside of the lid. Beneath the MOD crest were the words: *Grenades. Fragmentation. High explosive. Type M78. Red band, standard five-second delay. Yellow band, fifteen-second extended delay.*

Hadn't the courier said the yellows could be as short as ten seconds and as long as twenty-five? She'd have to take a chance. There was no alternative.

The clumping of heavy boots and the whimper of a protesting voice began to echo out of the long passageway that led to the kitchen at the rear of the house. The sound grew louder, then Nathan burst into the entrance hall, dragging the man called Pepe. A handcuff was still attached to the Colombian's ankle. It jingled as they crossed the marble floor.

Samantha looked into Nathan's face. 'Lift the bar and open the door when I nod. When Zarina comes, let her in, then close the door, drive the bolts and drop the bar.' She touched his cheek. He nodded to show he'd understood.

She hooked her fingers over Pepe's collar, made him walk backwards, shuffling and staggering, towards the table. One of his eyes was blackened and closed, his unshaven face bruised and gashed, his hair matted. He reeked of blood and vomit.

Keeping his back to the table, she settled three red-banded grenades in the hood of his anorak, then picked up a fourth, one with a yellow band. After drawing the pin, she pressed it into the palm of the hand holding his collar, ready to be dropped into the hood. Her hands were small. They were shaking. She had to keep the detonating lever depressed, but its spring was strong, making the grenade difficult to hold.

She pushed Pepe over to the door, put the muzzle of the gun against his temple and nodded at Nathan. He drew the bolts, lifted the bar, and she propelled her hostage out on to the paved area at the top of the steps.

They stood together, blinking in the blinding glare of the headlights as she called out, 'You there, Renato? This is your son. Pepe. Give me the child and I'll give you your son.'

'Liar!' roared the gruff voice. 'Pepe is in London, with Ricardo, doing business. Julio and Daman are here, beside me. I have no other sons.'

'Take a closer look, Renato.' She jabbed Pepe with the gun and muttered, 'Tell him who you are.'

'It's me, Father, Pepe. This is one hell of a crazy bitch. She shot Ricardo and left him to die. When Hueco and Harman didn't turn up, Ricardo said we should come here, find them, recover the stuff. She caught us breaking into the car.'

The scent of blood on his clothes had roused the dogs to a frenzy of howling and barking. Almost blinded by the lights of the cars, Samantha could make out no more than teeth and snarling mouths; the red gleam of blood in the retinas at the backs of their eyes. Their handlers were heaving on chains and yelling curses, struggling to maintain control of the slavering beasts.

Father and sons drew close and huddled together, debating what to do. Samantha's hand was wet with perspiration. She could feel the grenade slipping free, its detonating lever lifting. 'The child,' she demanded. 'Release her to me and you can have your son. If you don't, I'll kill him. What will you tell his mother then, Renato? That you behaved like a big man and it was just too bad it lost her a son?' She bit her lip until she could taste blood. Her hand was shaking, her stomach churning with terror. She was losing her grip on the grenade. The lever was lifting. It was slipping free.

Yelling so he could be heard above the yelping and snarling of the dogs, Renato said, 'You'll pay for this. You and everyone in that house.' He glanced at the man holding Zarina. 'Let her go.' The man lifted her to the ground, she began to run, but he caught her hair and held her back.

'Bring Pepe to the foot of the steps,' Renato demanded. 'Julio, take the girl over.'

The grenade had almost slipped out of her hand. She pushed it hard against the back of Pepe's neck, struggling to keep the detonator depressed as she urged him forward. The son called Julio took Zarina by the arm and led her across the forecourt.

Samantha pointed the gun at Julio, allowed the grenade to fall amongst the others in the hood of Pepe's anorak, then shoved him into the arms of his brother. She dragged Zarina up the steps and hurled her towards the door. A hairy arm reached out and drew her inside. Samantha fell to her knees, crawled to the edge of the landing and lowered herself into the shadows. Eight, nine, ten . . . Counting heartbeats, she stood on her tiptoes and risked a glance over the stonework. A father was embracing his wounded son; the boy's brothers were joining in . . . Eleven, twelve, thirteen . . . Would the thing never detonate?

A guttural voice yelled, 'Unleash a dog.' A man knelt down, a chain rattled, a chorus of male voices began to chant, 'Kill the bitch, kill the bitch,' and a snarling black shape hurtled across the forecourt. Gun raised, crouching behind the stonework, Samantha waited. Suddenly the bared teeth and slobbering jaws, the massive head and sleek black body appeared and bounded down the side of the steps towards her. She squeezed the trigger. A great weight of hot, hairy, bleeding flesh crashed into her and sent her sprawling back against the wall of the house.

Light blazed, blue and blinding. A pain that was unbelievably intense lanced her ears, a crushing force battered her brain and body.

Dazed and trembling, she eventually began to hear sounds: distorted, muffled, meaningless; faint echoes that reached her as if from a great distance. Something warm and wet was lying across her chest, something hard was pressing into her back. When she raised herself into a sitting position, the Heckler swung against her thigh, the body of the dog rolled down to her legs. She heaved it aside, staggered to her feet, then raised her head above the steps. All but three of the car headlights had been extinguished, and the screams and moans of men, the howls and yelping of dogs, were rising from the wreckage.

Body shaking, face and hair smeared with the dog's blood and saliva, she began to search in the darkness for her automatic pistol.

* * *

Nurse Stockwell lay, trembling, on threadbare carpet. From beyond the shattered windows she could hear dogs howling; men moaning, crying out for help in languages she couldn't understand. She'd been lying there for quite a while, holding her breath, fearing another explosion.

She crawled out from behind Alexander's bed, rose to her feet and took his pulse. It was normal. His breathing was a little shallow, but nothing to give concern. She stepped over to the window and drew a curtain aside. Shards of glass cascaded down to the floor; the lined velvet had captured the flying fragments. Down in the forecourt, a woman was clambering over the tangled wreckage of cars and vans. She would take a few paces, pause, raise the gun, then its thundering crash would echo around the forecourt and roll out across the woods. One by one, the men fell silent; the dogs ceased their howling.

Someone squeezed into the embrasure beside her. She turned. A tearful Zarina was staring up at her. 'Georgie . . . is Georgie all right?' The child peered through the window. 'She's there. Look, she's holding her gun. She's — '

Josie Stockwell drew her away from the window and let the curtain fall back.

'What's she doing?' Zarina demanded.

'Tying up loose ends. Go and tell your mother Alexander's safe and everything's over. Georgie won't be long.'

* * *

'You're looking a bit under the weather, Marcus.' Loretta Fallon dropped her briefcase and sank into the visitor's chair.

He managed a tired smile. 'Had a call from Quest in the early hours. Been an assault on Sourbeck Hall: the Lujans, father and sons, plus hired hands and dogs. And two Egyptians were in the party, both state security. Sixteen men and a dozen dogs in all. They demanded Alexander.'

'And?'

'Quest was already holding one of Lujan's sons; had him locked in a laundry room.' He glanced at his notes: 'Pepe. Cut a long story short, there was a confrontation on the entrance steps; Quest put three grenades in the hood of Pepe's anorak, dropped in a fourth and sent him over to join the family. Not much left of the Lujans. Remaining men and dogs no longer fit to fight. She searched the wreckage and the surrounding woods, killed all survivors, human and canine. They'd seen her, of course, lit by all the headlamps. She couldn't let them live. The gang injured one of the guards: fractured skull. He's in hospital, recovering.'

'Has she debriefed Alexander yet? I'm getting one hell of a battering. I can't — '

Marcus held up papers bound in blue covers. 'I took a chopper to the Hall. Quest handed over Alexander's notes. Very comprehensive, very detailed. There's a number of maps, too.'

'Thank God for that.' Loretta relaxed back in the chair. The hem of her navy-blue pencil skirt didn't quite cover her knees. Her matching jacket was short, its sleeves tight, its shoulders well padded. Her white silk blouse had a high collar. Marcus gazed at her across his cluttered desk. She'd never been a beautiful woman: her features were too large, her expression too cold and severe for that. But poise and a formidable intelligence made her very attractive, and the breasts beneath the blouse were generous; the legs under the skirt long and shapely. Above all, it was the aura of authority that captivated him. She radiated it. He found that immensely arousing.

He blinked the sleep from his eyes and stifled a yawn. 'I thought it wise to have Villiers at the Foreign Office look through it all before we copy it on to the Americans. There could well be material there we wouldn't wish them to see.'

Loretta nodded. 'And how's Quest?'

'Exhausted. I've moved in a team to clear up the mess; sent a lorry-load of old wooden pallets. There's a disused quarry on the estate. I told them to make a pyre and cremate the bodies — men and dogs, then shovel the ashes into a pool that fills the lower levels.'

'And the two Egyptians: do you think they were able to get a message out?'

'We were intercepting interesting traffic throughout the day. I thought something might be happening, so I had the mobile phone mast that serves the valley disabled. No messages got out. Quest had to drive three miles before she could put a call through.'

'So, no traces, we have Alexander's notes, and no one knows a thing. A good outcome, Marcus. And where's your beautiful little killer now?'

'Probably reached home.' He shuffled through papers. 'She's made an unusual request.'

Loretta Fallon gave him one of her cool looks.

'The courier took a nearly new black Volvo from the pool when he drove down to collect the embassy car. Quest wants it to be given to a man who works at the hall: a deaf mute. He's compellingly ugly.'

'She'll have her reasons. Write it off as crash damaged. I'll authorize the disposal. What have we been paying her?'

'Highest contract rate.'

'Extend her contract by six months, but don't call her in, just pay her.' Loretta picked up her case and rose to her feet. When she reached the door, she turned and looked back at him. 'How many men did you say there were, Marcus?'

'Sixteen, seventeen if we include the man she was holding hostage, and six fighting dogs. And she eliminated four other intruders. More than twenty men in all.'

'It was a massacre, Marcus.' She continued to hold him in her cool grey stare.

He smiled sleepily. 'Wholesale slaughter.'

'I must stop calling her your beautiful little killer. It's so condescending, so demeaning. After all, we're both sisters engaged in the great struggle.'

'The great struggle, ma'am? Presumably you mean the defence of the realm and its institutions?'

'Much more than that, Marcus. Civilization's being engulfed by a great wave of darkness. That's what we're really battling against.'

Marcus pondered for a moment, then his face brightened. 'How about Sister Slaughter? Perhaps we should call her Sister Slaughter.'

Loretta laughed. 'That's not quite what I had in mind, Marcus, but it's most appropriate. Just between us, though. It must go no further.'

14

Helen Wallace glanced around the crowded salon. It looked strangely bare without the curtains, and the naked windows were letting in too much of the autumn sunlight, exposing the shabbiness of a room full of memories, a room that often featured in her dreams.

Rasha had taken the priest's arm. She was walking him along the buffet, helping him to choose delicacies. A new housekeeper was hovering. Two maids from the catering firm were carrying trays of drinks, offering them to the academics and their wives who'd come to pay their last respects to a colleague and friend.

Howard was being especially kind, being avuncular, to Maria and Amir, pouring orange juice into glasses, getting them things their small arms couldn't reach. Children liked him. His pupils adored him. Audiences gave him standing ovations for his amateur theatricals. Pity he hadn't been able to devote a little more time to her.

Nathan was sitting on the big sofa, wearing a very smart suit and an expensive-looking shirt and tie. His foxy hair had been tamed by a skilful barber; his black shoes gleamed. That woman was sitting next to him, the one sent by Alexander's friend to mind the house. What was her name? Grey . . . Georgina Grey. And Zarina was there, too; deftly moving her hands and fingers, helping them to converse in the language of the deaf. Such a strange child. She gave one such knowing looks. She and the black-haired woman were a pair. They both had disturbing eyes. They were like a couple of witches.

When the black-haired woman had joined the procession to the mausoleum she'd sidled up to Nathan, slid her arm through his and kissed him. God, it had made her want to vomit! How could she bring herself to even touch the creature? If Mummy could see him now, sitting on her sofa, in her best room, she'd turn in her grave.

'Brought you some chicken, love; bit of salad, a few vol-au-vents. That okay?' Howard settled the plate on the arm of her chair, handed her a knife and fork wrapped in a napkin, then perched on a stool beside her. 'Who's the woman in the little black dress and high heels, sitting next to Nathan?'

'Someone sent by a friend of Alexander to look after the place while Rasha was in hospital.'

He cut into a roll. 'Rasha seems fine now,

and she's coping with the death rather well.' He forked in ham, added some salad, then took another look at Alexander's widow. Her hair had been gathered up, diamonds glittered on her ears and around her throat, her splendid breasts were shapely beneath a black woollen dress. When she turned and led the bearded priest over to a chair, its full skirt swirled around her long dancer's legs. Howard bit into the roll, then mumbled, 'She had old Alexander shriven.'

'Try not to talk with your mouth full, Howard. Shriven?'

'Confessed his sins to the priest; given absolution, the last rites, the whole works. Zarina told me.'

Helen let out a laugh of amazement. 'Alexander, confessed his sins? I don't believe it.'

He took another bite. 'It's true. She said he died in her mother's arms; just fell asleep.' Howard chuckled. 'Cleansed and comforted. Clever old Alexander.' He took his eyes off Rasha; allowed them to wander around the room. Suddenly he frowned. 'Something's changed, Helen. The old place doesn't look the same any more.'

'Rasha's had the curtains taken down and draped over the great frieze in the mausoleum. And God knows where she got that life-size crucifix. Did they have to make the figure so real? Blood and teeth and anguished eyes; they'd even given it eyelashes and hair. It was utterly obscene. And Grandfather's statue of Isis and Horus had been taken away and that crowned Virgin and Child put in its place. And there was that battered old statue of Saint Anthony where Anubis had been. It was all so unspeakably florid and Roman, Howard. That vulgar little Philistine has vandalized the place.'

'Spanish,' Howard mumbled. He chewed and swallowed. Mmm . . . very decent ham, this: thick and succulent and sweet. Rasha knew how to lay on a buffet.

'Spanish?'

'The crucifix and statues.' He was dispensing knowledge, imparting facts. It was something he did all day in classrooms filled with fresh-faced teenage girls. He couldn't stop himself. 'Probably nineteenth century,' he went on. 'They went in for extreme realism. Chucked out of some convent, I expect. Rasha's Coptic Christian. It's what she's used to. Orthodox: heavy on the liturgy, not so taken up with the dogma, very keen on statues and icons.' He chuckled. 'And you've got to hand it to her, she got old Alexander to embrace the faith and make his last confession, gave him a peaceful death. Good for her.'

'His first confession,' Helen retorted.

'Whatever. It's still one of life's mysteries.' He rose to his feet. 'I'm going to get some more of that ham and another roll. Can I get you anything?'

'You can bring me a cup of tea.' She watched him stride over to the big slab-sided sofa and introduce himself to the black-haired woman with the green eyes and bright-red lips — he wouldn't be able to resist chatting to her. He said something that made her smile and Zarina giggle, then shook Nathan's hand before launching himself off towards the buffet table.

Helen closed her eyes. She suddenly felt like an intruder in a house she still thought of as her home; a place where things were being changed, the comforting and the familiar cast aside. She remembered going with her mother to London, to Harrods, where they'd chosen the silk brocade for the curtains. Yards and yards of it. She remembered her feelings of awe and wonder when she'd gone inside Grandfather's mausoleum, with its huge mural and the gilded statues of the gods. The mural was hidden behind curtains now. The statues had been carted away. Everything spoiled and robbed of its meaning. And Alexander had betrayed them. He'd embraced the faith of his wife, confessed his sins, probably to the priest who was talking to Rasha and her two youngest children at this very moment.

Confession: all stain of sin wiped clean; the leaden weight of guilt removed. It was done in a particular way. There was a procedure, a sort of formula. She'd read about it once. You said, 'Bless me, Father, for I have sinned,' then you told him how long it was since your last confession and began to recount your miserable little faults and failings. Priests must be bored senseless, shut up in that little box, listening to the same old drivel, hour after hour.

She wouldn't bore him. She'd make him sit up and take notice. 'I have coveted my sister-in-law's house and possessions, I have born false witness against her, had her incarcerated with the insane, her children taken away from her and given to strangers, denied my dying brother the comfort of their company. And I have lain with a man who was not my husband, a husband for whom I feel nothing but contempt.'

He'd ask her how many times. She'd absolutely no idea. Twice in motels, many times in his home: on the stairs, on the sofa, on the rug, in his bed. Should she tell the priest that some of the things they'd done together had been quite depraved; that after a shamefully short time she'd no longer tried to resist, that she'd begun to crave the man's attentions? Even when he'd told her the local health authority had compelled him to release Rasha, she'd continued to meet him.

The priest would have to deny her absolution. She felt no remorse, no shame. Whilst the affair had lasted she'd felt only excitement, euphoria, an ecstatic release. Now it was over, now he no longer called her, she felt lonely and depressed.

She'd first heard about it in the morning paper, a brief and restrained account of a Dr Asadi, a psychiatrist, found murdered in his home. The Sunday papers had been more explicit. He'd been found naked, spread-eagled across his bed, his hands and ankles secured to the bedposts by four pairs of handcuffs. First reports had said he'd bled to death. By Sunday they'd carried out an autopsy, and the papers were able to reveal that he'd been asphyxiated. His genitals — penis, scrotum, everything — had been hacked away and stuffed into his mouth. He'd choked to death on his own bits and pieces. The article mentioned his flight from danger in Iraq and hinted at revenge, but it would seem the police were baffled by the crime. Who could have done an unspeakable thing like that to such a gentle and caring man?

Howard was approaching with a heaped

plate. He really was quite stupid. He'd taken so much weight off to act the part of Heathcliff and now he was piling it all back on again.

He settled himself on his stool and handed her the cup of tea. 'You seem upset, love. I think you're more upset about Alexander than you'd care to admit.'

'I'd be lying if I said I was, Howard. I'm upset about all the things I've lost.'

He put his arm around her shoulders. She shrugged it away. Undeterred, he said softly, 'It's just a decaying old house, love; full of shabby things. Would we want the worry of it all?'

'You've never been into the storeroom, Howard. Some of the things in there are worth a fortune.' She sipped her tea, then rattled the cup down on its saucer. Her hands were shaking. 'And it's not just the house. It's all the other things I've lost.' She bowed her head and began to weep.

'I can't think what you mean, love. We still have one another, we have Timothy and Harriet. We've got our home; we're comfortable and as secure as anyone can be these days. Is it because Timothy's going to university? Are you upset about him leaving?'

She shook her head.

He leaned forward and kissed her, very

gently, on the cheek. 'You know I love you, don't you, Helen? You're everything to me. You make everything I do worthwhile. I don't know what I'd do if you — '

Tears began to bucket down. 'Why are you saying all this now?' she sobbed. 'Why didn't you say it that first time I drove down to see Alexander? Even if you'd just said, 'I miss you,' or 'I'd rather you didn't stay,' or 'I want you to come home,' it would have been enough.'

Perplexed now, he said, 'I can't think what's got into you, Helen. This is so unlike you. What's the — '

'God, you can be so stupid, Howard,' she hissed. 'You, with your first from Oxford, endlessly airing your precious knowledge, when all the time you know absolutely nothing about anything that really matters. You're a fool, and I loathe and despise you.'

She flung the words into his startled face, then leaped up and ran from the room, along the passageway that led to the hall and out through the front door.

Leaves rustled under her feet as she wandered across the forecourt. Great drifts of them had gathered: red, yellow, brown, gold, their autumn colours glowing in the soft light of the late-afternoon sun. She realized then that she would never return to her childhood home again.

Back in the salon, Howard was discreetly glancing at the other mourners. No one seemed to have noticed; no one had heard Helen's outburst. He couldn't believe it. This was so unlike her. She was probably more upset about her brother than she realized. He'd leave her alone for a while, give her a chance to calm down, then go and see where she'd got to. He bit into his roll. Such succulent ham, and the wine was full-bodied and smooth, not some fiver-a-bottle plonk. Rasha had never been stingy. And she was looking wonderful, sexier than ever. And Zarina was growing up: very pretty, very demure, in that grey dress with the white collar and cuffs. She was going to be a beauty, like her mother. Alexander had been a lucky old devil.

* * *

Zarina was strolling across the forecourt with Samantha. They were heading towards the two remaining cars. Uncle Howard and a tearful Aunt Helen had already left; her mother was saying goodbye to the priest.

She glanced up at Samantha. 'That man you sent, the one who measured Nathan for the suits: he was very nice. He said he came from a place called Saville Row. Where's that?'

'It's a street in London, where the very best men's clothes are sold.'

'He didn't look the least bit shocked when he saw Nathan, and he was awfully polite. He kept saying, 'Would sir mind holding out his arm; would sir like this or that.' I did the sign language for them, and Mummy helped choose the shirts and ties and shoes. And that big black car belongs to Nathan now. We start school next week. Mummy's found us a new one. Nathan's going to take us there and bring us back in it.' She slid her hand into Samantha's. 'Will you come and see me again?'

'I don't think so.'

'Why not? I should like it so very much.'

'I'm dangerous to know.' Samantha's husky voice was soft and wistful. 'Bit like Alexander, really. In the end, the things he knew made him a danger to you all.' She clicked open her bag, took out one of the cards engraved with *Georgina Grey Investigations,* and wrote a number on the back. She handed it to Zarina. 'Keep that safe. It's my private number. No one else has it.'

'Not even Crispin?'

'Not even Crispin. If you need me, and you must really need me, call it, and I'll come to you.' She opened the door of the Ferrari.

'Where are you going now?'

'To Brighton. Crispin's waiting for me

there. Then we're crossing over to France and driving down to Italy.'

'For a holiday?'

'Sort of. I'm searching for clothes: Paris, Milan, Rome; we might spend a week in Venice.'

'Has he kissed you yet?'

Samantha smiled. 'Not yet.'

'He must be incredibly shy.'

She lowered herself behind the wheel, then drew Zarina close and held her tight, reflecting, once again, that a child like this might have been hers. 'I'll miss you,' she whispered, then kissed her and let her go.

'I'll miss you heaps.'

Samantha slammed the door and lowered the window. 'No more spells.'

'Mummy's burned the grimoires.'

She started the engine, revved it, then squeezed Zarina's hand. 'Work hard at school: that's what Alexander would have wanted. And always do as your mother says.'

'I'll try. Bye, Georgie.'

Samantha let out the clutch and roared off down the drive, snatching glances in the mirrors at the receding figure of the dusky, dark-eyed girl in the grey dress. She was still waving.